TRAPPED SPIRIT

TRAPPED SPIRIT

RESTLESS SPIRITS, BOOK 3

AMY RAVENEL

FALSTAFF
BOOKS
WWW.FALSTAFFBOOKS.COM

To Rachel and Susan. You're the best besties a girl could ever have.

W hen you made a deal with the devil, he always came to collect. Or at least that's how Tabitha Lawson saw it as she waited beside a lake in the dark in early March.

Groaning, she draped her camera around her neck, slid open the white van's door, and stepped into the cold air. Her booted feet crunched in the icy grass. The days warmed in early spring in Asheville, but the nights were still too chilly for her. She sucked in a breath as the cold touched her face.

She regretted agreeing to this entire investigation. She clicked on her flashlight and made her way down to the lake. She hated being back at Laureline Lake. The place made her skin crawl, nothing surrounding it but trees, and she credited it as the beginning of her fractured relationship with her older sister, Lisa Greene.

"Isn't this the best weather ever?" Drew Keane pointed his phone at Tabitha. Bundled from head to toe, he wore his favorite Duke Blue Devils cap over a black wool hat that covered his blondish-brown hair. Delight sparkled in his hazel-green eyes. He held a black case carrying a camera in his other hand. As the man in charge of the technology at Restless Spirits, he knew where to place the cameras and other equipment for the upcoming investigation.

"I beg to differ." Tabitha shivered. She didn't know why anyone would enjoy the cold weather.

She brushed off his cheerfulness and returned her thoughts to the night's investigation. She didn't resent the idea behind the case she had agreed to take. Two nights before, a teenaged girl named Monica had camped with her friends near the lake, and she had disappeared without a trace. Lisa brought the case to Tabitha's attention. Tabitha wanted to turn it down—she hated the idea of going back to Laureline Lake—but then, Lisa called in her favor. A favor Tabitha regretted offering to her.

Two months earlier, Drew fought a family curse that almost claimed his life. To fight off a killer shadow, he built a device that broke apart a ghost's energy, his trusty Ghost Disruptor. It resembled a laser gun out of a cheesy science fiction movie. However, he didn't have all the parts he needed, and the missing one cost too much money. Lisa owned that missing part at The Greene Institute for Paranormal Research, a large facility located in Charlotte that Tabitha's family owned and operated. She had given it to Drew in exchange for a favor, and to save her friend, Tabitha agreed to the deal, too.

Stuffing one of her gloved hands into the pocket of her coat, Tabitha searched the wooded area for her husband. She found him a few trees away with their two other co-workers, the resident psychics on the team and sometimes annoying love birds, McKenna Ellison and Tristan Johnson.

She scrunched her nose as the cold wind bit her cheeks and walked over to the three. "What's going on over here?"

"Just going over some rules. I don't want your sisters to know about Mac and Tristan." Aaron gave Tristan a pointed look. "And I'm hoping Tristan here can manage his power."

"Dude, I'm twenty-five, not five. I can handle it." Tristan narrowed his green eyes, the only body part visible. He wrapped the rest of his head in a scarf. A few wayward curls escaped and rested on his golden forehead.

McKenna pushed her long, brown hair out of her face, her sky blue eyes bright. "We've been practicing," she protested.

"You a bit cold there, man?" Drew asked as he joined them and pointed at Tristan.

Tristan glared at him. "You know how I feel about the cold."

Drew chuckled. "I do. I spent most of our childhood dragging you out to play in the snow."

Aaron rubbed his gloved hands together and searched the area. "Tabby, where are your sisters?"

"They're coming. Corrie called a few minutes ago and said they were about fifteen minutes away." She jumped up and down, trying to stay warm. Everything inside of her screamed that this whole thing was a bad idea.

"I wish they'd hurry," Aaron glared in the direction of the gravel road that connected them to civilization.

"You and me both." She wanted to get this over with before her feet froze.

"Maybe we can go ahead? We can get a feel for the place before your sisters get here." McKenna suggested. "At least we can walk around and get our blood moving." She huddled next to Tristan, her hands shoved into the pockets of her puffy coat.

"Good idea," Tabitha agreed. She really wanted to be back in the Restless Spirits van with the heat running. Even better, back in her own bed under her own blankets in her own heated house. Anywhere but that cursed lake. Nothing good ever happened in that place.

McKenna, Tristan, and Drew headed off to the right while Tabitha and Aaron headed left.

As they walked around the still, quiet body of water, Tabitha switched her camera to night mode and snapped pictures. The moonlight shone through the naked branches of the trees, bathing the wooded area around the lake in a soft light. The branches framed the moon, making it the centerpiece of the scene. Tabitha couldn't resist. She angled her camera toward the treetops and clicked the shutter several times. She took the shot from several different angles.

"I don't think the ghost is in the trees." Aaron walked up behind her, a flashlight in one gloved hand and a small black box called an electromagnetic field detector in the other. The needle inside the tiny window on the electromagnetic field detector remained unmoving while the lights on top stayed dark.

Tabitha lowered the camera and flipped through the pictures. Some of them didn't turn out the way she wanted, but others appeared sharp and clear. They told a story, the moon casting an eerie glow through the trees and on the still water. With a little photoshopping, they might be excellent additions to her portfolio. "These aren't for the hunt."

She felt him hover over her shoulder. "They look great."

"Thank you." She moved away from him, her eyes on the quiet, dark lake.

"Tabby, what's wrong? You've been quiet for the last couple of weeks." Aaron reached her in two strides. Not hard to do since he towered over her by eight inches. His legs were much longer.

She shrugged and kept walking. She hoped he hadn't noticed her change in mood, and she didn't really want to talk about it. She had been thinking about her career and what she wanted her future to look like. How could she tell him she wanted this to be her last paranormal investigation?

"I'm fine," she said.

Aaron stepped in front of her, stopping her progress. He peered down at her, his brown eyes soft in the dimming light. Tabitha loved his eyes. They had little flecks of gold in them. He looked like an Eskimo all bundled in his thick coat, hat, and gloves, covering all of his tanned skin. Short sprigs of straight brown hair peeked out from beneath the dark gray wool hat.

"You're not fine. You haven't been fine for a while now. Something's bothering you." He took one of her hands. "You can always talk to me."

"It's nothing, really." She pulled her hand out of his. "Now isn't the time. We have a ghost to find, right?" She stepped around him and kept walking.

She loved Aaron, and she worried her news would break his heart. They had been together for three years, married for two. When she first met him on an investigation involving a ghost haunting a bed and breakfast, he acted arrogant and chatty. But as the night drew to a close, after getting locked in a room together, he had softened, and she started to warm up to him. By the end of the investigation, she found herself saying yes to a date.

His life involved investigating ghosts. She used to share his passion until the past year. Seeing ghosts almost take the lives of her team, her friends, terrified her. Before Restless Spirits, she had encountered one other ghost who killed. She'd never forget the damage the spirit left in its wake. She never expected to fight two more deadly ghosts. She had investigated the paranormal her whole life, and she desperately wanted a change. Something safer and not so dark.

And she reached the problem. She never had a special

talent for hunting ghosts. She didn't even really have a special job at the agency. McKenna and Tristan used their psychic powers, Drew constructed the machines, and Aaron led them all. She helped with research and took pictures. Not even the pictures she wanted to take. She wanted to capture professional images that didn't involve dust masquerading as mysterious orbs.

But she practiced ways to tell Aaron. None of the words came out right. Not when she saw his face light up every time they helped a wayward ghost find peace. So, she kept walking and didn't say anything.

"Tabby, come on. We've got plenty of time. When have you ever known a ghost to be on time?" Aaron kept pace with her.

She stopped and sighed. "Well, I've been trying to figure out how to tell you."

"Tell me what?" A worried note crept into his voice. "You're not leaving me, are you?"

"What?" Tabitha chuckled a little. "No." She touched his cheek. "Never. You're stuck with me, big boy." She dropped her hand back to her side. "I...I don't want to investigate ghosts anymore."

Aaron stopped walking. "You don't?"

"I don't." Tabitha faced him.

"Why?" His features were barely visible between the flashlight and the moonlight, but Tabitha made out the confusion in his voice.

Tabitha swallowed. Different reason flitted through her mind. *Because I'm scared. Because I've seen people die and almost lost a few more. Because my heart isn't in it anymore. Because you don't need me.* She settled on, "I need a change."

"Then what do you want to do?"

Tabitha cradled her camera in her hands, hoping it would steady her. "I found a job with a local travel magazine.

Western NC. It's full of photographs of the mountains and the trees and the towns. They're looking for a new photographer. I think I'd be good at it."

Her eyes had adjusted enough to the low light that she saw Aaron smile. "Of course, you'd be great at it. So, do you need to cut down to weekends? A couple of hours through the week? We can work with this."

"Aaron, I want to walk away completely, focus on the photography."

Aaron took a step back, his smile fading. "But we're in this together. It's our dream."

"It's your dream, and I support it a hundred percent. But I want to follow my dream, and I don't think investigating the paranormal is it."

Aaron opened his mouth to answer when another voice cut through the night.

"You started without us?" Lisa waved her hands, her disbelief loud enough to frighten any animal in the vicinity.

"We'll talk about this when we get home, okay?" Aaron clutched his equipment and walked away, not waiting for an answer.

Tabitha turned to find two flashlights bobbing in their direction. As they grew closer, she made out two figures bundled in coats and hats. Lisa, the taller of the two, had a scowl on her pale face. She wore her blonde hair loose, and the straight locks fell to her shoulders. Unlike everyone else, she wore a leather jacket. Tabitha thought that she had to be freezing, but Lisa didn't seem to mind it. Her eyes, royal blue like Tabitha's, flashed with anger.

Corrie jogged behind her, bundled head to toe in winter gear. She looked as if she were going on a ski trip. She had tied her long hair, blonde like her sisters', back into a low ponytail. Worry hovered in her own royal blue eyes.

Three blonde and blue-eyed ghost hunters, back together

again. For a moment, Tabitha wished she had died her hair completely purple.

She tabled Aaron's anger. She planned to deal with one problem at a time, and Lisa was the most immediate.

Tabitha raised her walkie-talkie to her lips to let the rest of the team know. "Lisa and Corrie are here. Meet you back at the van."

"IT'S BAD ENOUGH YOU BROUGHT YOUR WHOLE TEAM, BUT YOU couldn't wait for us?" Lisa threw her hands in the air as her voice raised an octave with each word. "We were only a couple of minutes late."

"You were twenty minutes late, and we weren't starting without you." It took effort for Tabitha to keep her voice even. "We were getting a feel for the place."

Lisa crossed her arms over her chest. "Right. I'm sure that's all you did." She glared at the rest of Tabitha's team. "We didn't need everybody up here. I only asked for you."

Tabitha tossed her head back and groaned. She tensed at the thought of another argument with her oldest sister. "After what happened last time, I thought it'd be good to have some back up." She pressed her back against the Restless Spirits van, cold seeping in past her coat. Its chipping white paint looked a little shabby next to the sleek black of the Institute van.

"What happened last time?" McKenna joined them, looking from one sister to the other.

"You've been here before?" Tristan stood beside her.

Drew adjusted his hat, and for once, reserved his snappy quip.

Tabitha sighed. "Yeah, we've investigated this place before."

"It's not a big deal." Aaron crossed his arms over his chest.

"Not a big deal?" Lisa poked a finger into Tabitha's chest. "She cost me the biggest investigation ever."

"That's enough, Lisa. We're all here, and that's all that matters." Corrie Parker, their middle sister, stepped between them. One gloved hand rested on Lisa's chest, while the other touched Tabitha's. She addressed Tabitha. "We've missed working with you, and I'm excited to do this as sisters again. I bet Lisa is, too."

"She has a funny way of showing it." Tabitha retorted.

Every time she and Lisa orbited each other, they fought. Nothing Tabitha did or said came across as good enough for her oldest sister. It had been that way for years, even before she and Aaron left the Institute. Corrie forever tried to make peace between them.

"I don't know about you," Drew raised his voice. "But I'd like to know all of the facts before we jump into this thing." He sidled next to Tabitha. "So, what's the dirt? What really happened?" He held up a video camera. "And remember, you can't lie under fake ghost oath."

"I didn't take an oath, Drew. And it's not funny." A headache bloomed right between Tabitha's eyes. Why did she agree to this again? The handle to Drew's disruptor poked out from his pocket, and she remembered how they all got into this mess. It had been worth it to save Drew's life.

If only he had enough parts to make them each a disruptor. But he owned the only prototype at the moment.

Tabitha groaned and shivered in the cold. She didn't want to tell the story to McKenna, Drew, and Tristan, but they deserved to know what happened. They thought they were there to investigate the legend of Laureline Lake, a legend involving a ghostly woman, a portal, and a missing teenager. She needed them to know there was more to the story.

She pushed away Drew's camera and cleared her throat.

"Four years ago, Lisa, Corrie, and I were a team. Dad's idea. Lisa is the tech genius, Corrie is the psychic muscle, and I'm everything else. Or I was."

2

Four years earlier

The setting sun glinted off the small lake, and the light reflected through the bare trees, giving the whole area a spooky feel. Tabitha couldn't resist. She lifted her camera to her eye and shot several atmospheric photographs. Something about the calm waters of Laureline Lake soothed her. The quiet, peaceful area had a comforting presence. The moonlight glinting off the water with the dark trees framing it made an amazing photograph. No wonder it was a hidden gem in the mountains. Tourists never visited. No companies built big houses boasting private docks. It was a small and quiet place with thick forest surrounding it. One gravel path led in and out of the area, and the county worked hard to keep it that way.

The legend also added to the mystery. Throughout the year, when the full moon rose, people claimed to see a solitary ghost walk along the water's edge. She was young, had flowing straight hair, and wore a sad expression on her face. She almost seemed like a regular person until one noticed the bluish-white glow around her. As soon as they realized it, she'd disappear.

But the ghost only told one part of the legend. On cold March nights with the full moon overhead, the legend said dancing lights sometimes grew into a portal. To where, no one knew. It might be to Heaven or to Hell or to somewhere else entirely. Nothing and no one exited it, but people vanished into it.

Most people never saw the portal. They camped out, saw nothing, and returned home with a funny story or two. But some people went missing at the lake. Local law enforcement never found any of the people that disappeared, but they mostly chalked it up to people running away. Nothing suggested foul play. The weird thing was no one ever heard from these people again.

These disappearances had been going on for forty years. Most years had none, but others had one or two people snatched away in the night. And if they ventured to the lake with friends, those friends all told the same story involving a bluish-white ghost and a portal.

Lisa had been fascinated with the legend for as long as Tabitha could remember. She suggested it to their father, Philip Greene, the head of The Greene Institute,. Her theory was that if people disappeared and left no body behind, then maybe the legend was true. Lisa wanted nothing more than to prove that.

Lisa had set up one of the Institute's sleek black vans with all of the latest monitors and computers. She planned to capture every bit of footage.

Corrie walked the lake, breathing evenly. She had the toughest job, and the rarest power. Corrie perceived souls and channeled ghosts, if the ghosts were willing and needed to say something. Their father called her a medium. Corrie couldn't predict when her power might work and when it might not. When it happened, the ghost inhabited her body for a short time and spoke through her. Corrie could receive crucial information that helped investigations. On a few occasions, Tabitha witnessed Corrie attempt to help the wayward souls, but Lisa would shut it down before Corrie could finish.

"Alright, the conditions are right." Lisa jumped out of the van holding a small video camera. "We've got the moon over-head, and we've got the three of us."

Tabitha lowered her digital camera. "Why does it matter that there's three of us?"

Lisa grinned. "Three is a sacred number, a magical number."

"Magical? You've been talking to Dad again, haven't you?" Tabitha looked away from her camera and lifted an eyebrow.

Lisa waved away her concerns. "I know it sounds like he's off his rocker when he says stuff like that, but we do make a pretty good team." She shrugged as she set a tripod beside the nearest tree. "Besides, it couldn't hurt, right?" She set a digital camera on the tripod and checked the angle.

Tabitha rolled her eyes but decided to leave it. She nodded in her middle sister's direction. "Corrie's over there. How do you want to do this?"

Lisa stepped back. "You take the right side, and I'll take the left." Lisa walked over to Corrie, and Tabitha followed.

"Hi, guys." Corrie smiled at them as they approached. "I feel open and ready." She bounced up and down, her hands stuffed in the pockets of her big coat.

"I need you here." Lisa pointed at a spot between the camera and the edge of the lake. "See if you can attract the ghost." Lisa fiddled with the video camera, checking to make sure she turned it on and that it filmed in the dark. Satisfied with her progress, she pulled out her small electromagnetic field detector and held it up. The needle and lights held steady. "Okay, you ready?"

"As I'll ever be," Tabitha mumbled. She readied her own equipment and set off to the right. The cold grass crunched under her booted feet, but the place remained otherwise quiet.

As per Institute policy, they researched the area as well as all the details about the ghost they could find. Tabitha found a newspaper clipping about a teenaged girl who drowned there in 1974, a girl named Amanda Perez. According to the article, the police ruled her death a tragic accident. But Tabitha thought there might be more to it since ghosts appeared after horrible intentional deaths, not accidents. A few other people had drowned at the lake throughout the years, but Amanda's death coincided with the stories about the portal.

The night stretched out before them, and hours passed. Tabitha snapped picture after picture of the lake, the trees, and the moon. But it seemed to be a whole lot of nothing. After a while, she made her way back to Corrie, who circled a small area and spoke to the night air.

"You can come to me. I'll give you a voice," she offered to no one.

"No luck, huh?" Tabitha asked.

Corrie shook her head. "None." She rubbed her gloved hands together. "I hope Noah remembered to ask Caitlyn to brush her teeth before bed."

Tabitha smiled. "I'm sure he did. How long has he known you sometimes work nights?"

"You're right." Corrie sighed. "I'm worrying too much again."

Tabitha didn't blame her. She knew her middle sister would rather be at home with her daughter than out on a lake pursuing a ghost.

Lisa marched along the path. "Where is she? It's almost midnight."

"Maybe tonight is not our night," Corrie suggested.

"I'm not ready to call it." Lisa gritted her teeth. Her blue eyes flashed in the moonlight. "She's here. I feel it."

"Lisa, it's getting late, and I'm freezing. I don't think..." Tabitha stopped talking when she saw Corrie sway out of the corner of her eye. "Corrie?"

Her middle sister didn't answer. Instead, she closed her eyes and continued to waver. Tabitha and Lisa pointed their flashlights at her. In the eerie light, she quit moving. Her whole tiny body stilled. Then her eyes snapped open.

"Get out of here!" she bellowed. "Go! All of you! Now!"

"Amanda? Are we speaking to Amanda?" Lisa took a step forward.

Corrie shoved her hard enough that Lisa's backside landed on the ground. "Leave, before it's too late." She stumbled, dropping to the ground next to Lisa.

"Corrie?" Tabitha crouched down and touched her sister's arm. She then reached over to check Lisa.

Both groaned as they tried to sit up.

The wind blew, whistling through the bare branches. The cold stung Tabitha's face, and she turned away. Slowly, she stood, bringing her sisters with her. Turning, she saw soft lights dance between two trees. They resembled fairy lights. The lights danced and twirled, faster and faster, until they were spinning in a circle. Tabitha let go of her sisters and took a step toward it. She reached out.

Then the wind kicked up speed, blowing toward the lights. It seemed to push her closer to the circle, which grew larger each time the lights rotated.

Right at the moment she almost touched the lights, an invisible force shoved Tabitha backward. She tumbled into the icy lake with a large splash. The cold cut to the bone.

Sputtering, Tabitha grabbed a hold of the bank and pulled herself out of the water. By the time all of her flopped onto the shore, the lights had disappeared, and the wind had died down.

Corrie helped her to her feet. Tabitha shivered, dripping wet, teeth chattering. She yanked her wet camera off her neck. Groaning, she realized she had ruined it. Corrie steered her to the van while Lisa ran to where the lights had been, begging them to come back.

———

Now

"LISA STILL THINKS IT'S MY FAULT WE MISSED THE PORTAL," Tabitha grumbled.

"It was your fault. You let go." Lisa gripped her equipment in her gloved hand. "And you owe me this."

"You really believe the portal exists?" Aaron asked as he helped Corrie carry some of their equipment.

"I know it does, and we're going to prove it tonight."

McKenna snuggled into Tristan. "And hopefully find Monica, too."

"Sure. Yeah. And find the missing girl." Lisa's eyes shone in the moonlight. "But the portal would be an amazing discovery." She set a tripod near the lake in the same spot from five years earlier and positioned a camera onto it. "But where do you think all of those disappearing people went? They say ghost portals can form near a body of water where a trauma happened. Whatever happened to Amanda had to be traumatic because a portal is here." She turned on the camera and checked the angle. "Legend says a portal is proceeded by ghost lights." She stepped back, leaving the camera running. It pointed at the woods instead of the lake. "We almost had proof until someone fell into the lake."

"You're lucky I didn't freeze that night." Tabitha shuddered when she thought about it. She remembered how wet and miserable she had been.

"Well, tonight, I want to catch that portal in action." Lisa dusted her gloved hands on her jeans. "It's March, and the moon is out, kids." She held out her hands. "Let's go."

3

Tabitha pushed her frustration down. The investigation didn't center on her or her relationship with her sister. She agreed to it to find Monica and help a sad ghost. Let Lisa focus on her portal. She wanted to concentrate on ending this and getting on with the rest of her life. If she assisted two souls on her last investigation, then it was worth it.

Drew cleared his throat, breaking the awkward silence that fell over the group. "So, the Laureline Lake portal is real?" He moved his camera a couple of inches away from Lisa's. Her camera hovered so close it nearly knocked Drew's into the lake.

"Yes." Lisa checked her equipment once more. "We saw it."

Out of the corner of her eye, Tabitha saw McKenna exchange a look with Tristan. "I heard portals are supposed to have an effect on psychics."

"They do." Corrie said, her voice light. "When I channel, it takes effort on my part. But when I channeled the ghost near that portal, it felt so easy. Absolutely no effort at all."

"Really?" Tristan asked.

Tabitha turned away from the conversation. She blew on her gloved hands and rubbed them together to warm them. When she saw Aaron stalk over to Lisa, she groaned.

"Aren't you forgetting something? Didn't your sister, as the ghost—who may or may not be a girl named Amanda—tell you to get out of here?" Aaron set the equipment he had been holding on the ground. His brows dipped. "I don't like this. I don't like it one bit. Pack it up, gang. We're going home."

"Go." Lisa shrugged. "All I need is my baby sister. We don't need the rest of your so-called team." She moved away from her camera, hands on her hips. She nodded at Tristan and McKenna. "What do you two do anyway?" When they didn't answer, she glared at Tabitha. "But you have to stay. You owe me, remember?"

"Yeah, I remember." Tabitha touched Aaron's arm, hoping to calm him down. "She's right. You can go if you want. I'll keep an eye out for Monica, and I'll be okay."

Aaron laid his gloved hand over hers, his bigger one engulfing her smaller one. "I'm not leaving you here alone. Besides, we still need to talk."

"Not here." Tabitha shook her head. "We'll talk when we get home."

"We're not going anywhere," McKenna declared. She pushed her long, brown hair behind her shoulders. "What do you need us to do, Lisa? Our specialty is research, since you asked, but we can pick up the slack in other places."

Tabitha's lips twitched. McKenna wasn't lying.

Drew opened the sliding door to the Restless Spirits' van. "Well, I, for one, am happy to monitor the whole thing from inside the safety of my van."

"Thank you for the support, Drew," Tristan mumbled.

"Any time." With that, he stepped in and closed the door with a loud, creaky click.

"Drew, you only get an hour. Then we switch!" Aaron roared.

Lisa smirked from her spot near the lake. "Love the professionalism of your team."

Aaron scowled. "There's still the matter of the missing teenager, Monica. She's the main reason we're here."

"So, you said. Look, you investigate your way. I'll investigate mine." Lisa shifted and held out her hand to Tabitha again. "Come on. Let's go. We've got to see if we can recreate the circumstances that opened the portal. Tabby, you stood in the middle, and Corrie settled on the other side of you."

"This is ridiculous. There's no guarantee the portal will open tonight. It doesn't run on a schedule." Tabitha turned to her middle sister. "Corrie, are you really going along with this? Wouldn't you rather be home with Caitlyn?"

Corrie sighed as she took Tabitha's hand. "I would, but it's at least worth seeing if we can make the portal open." She wrinkled her nose as she smiled. "It's kind of exciting." She craned her neck to look up at her brother-in-law. "Aaron, I knew about that missing girl, and the portal might be the answer. When I channeled the ghost, she was adamant that we stay away." Her face became thoughtful. "She felt worried, afraid. Something important must be on the other side of that portal."

"What does Dad stand to gain if we open this thing?" Tabitha finally voiced the question nagging at the back of her mind. The Institute never investigated a haunting or an unexplained event unless her father benefited from it in some way. If they found a psychic, he'd create some way to recruit them. If they stumbled upon a ghost, he'd figure out some way to study it while keeping it on this plane of existence. Philip Greene had no interest in helping anyone but himself and his need for research.

Lisa groaned. "We're going to rehash that old argument?"

She approached Tabitha. "This isn't about Dad. This is my investigation, our investigation. It's about us working together again. Tabitha, you said you'd do this."

Tabitha took a breath. Lisa was right. She'd made a promise, and she kept stalling. She studied the dark trees in front of them, remembering the swirl of the lights as the portal pulled her in. A sense of wrongness had flashed through her mind. She had wanted to scream, to run, but she had kept moving toward it. Was that how Monica had felt? Had she been able to cry out for help? Tabitha didn't want to repeat the experience, but she had no choice. Lisa would badger her until she got her way.

Tabitha looked back at the rest of her team, who shivered next to the vans. The longer they fought about this, the more time everyone had to stand out in the cold.

"Fine." Tabitha met Lisa halfway. "My team can stake out the perimeter and see if they spot the ghost." She looked pointedly at McKenna and Tristan. "Or see if they pick up anything else." She turned back to Lisa. "I'll stay here with you." She moved between her sisters and took each of their hands.

"Good." Lisa led her back to the spot beside the lake. They faced the forest with the lake at their backs.

"Now what?" Tabitha asked. She felt like an idiot. "Should we say something?"

"Now." Lisa paused for a moment. "We wait."

AARON DETESTED THIS: HIS WIFE HOVERING BESIDE LAURELINE Lake at night with her sisters trying to make a ghost portal open. He called the whole idea ridiculous. It was beyond ridiculous. And what if that portal opened? Lisa wanted to see what the other side offered. Did she plan on jumping in?

Was she taking Tabitha and Corrie with her? Not if he had anything to say about it.

But what if Tabitha wanted to go, like she wanted to leave Restless Spirits? How could he just let her go? They'd started the business together. They were in this together. How could he stop her? Why would he stop her? Couples worked separate jobs all the time. No big deal. But what if a separate job led to other separate things, and Tabitha realized she wanted to do better than Aaron altogether?

He shoved that worry aside. He didn't have time to dwell on it, not while his investigation involved a ghost, a portal, and a missing girl he wanted to save. He needed to focus. He and Tabitha promised to talk later.

Clutching the electromagnetic field detector in one hand and his flashlight in the other, he gathered McKenna and Tristan. Drew monitored everything from inside the van. Tabitha and her sisters continued to stare at the dark trees in total, creepy silence. He felt his walkie-talkie in his pocket, ready in case anything happened.

Aaron took his team around the right side of the lake, walking around the curve of the bank. He glanced behind him to see Tabitha and her sisters across the water. "Okay, we're far enough away over here. If you two pick up anything, let me know. Tristan, if you can definitely tell me who this ghost is and what happened to her, I'll give you a bonus."

"If what Corrie said was true, my control might go either way." Tristan shivered. "But I'll try."

"It's going to be okay." McKenna squeezed his hand. "If you get extra control, I'll get extra control. I'll be here to help you out."

Aaron tuned them out and held out the EMF detector. The needle hadn't moved, and the lights hadn't brightened since they got there. It made sense. No houses or electrical lights were anywhere near the lake. Still, that meant if the ghost or the portal made an appearance, Aaron hoped he'd be the first to know.

He watched Tabitha across the lake. She had let go of Lisa and had her arms wrapped around her body. They seemed to be arguing again. He shook his head and sighed. They fought like that before Aaron ever asked Tabitha out, and it got worse when she agreed to marry him. The arguments seemed to grow worse every year.

He counted his lucky stars every day that she married him. Until Tabitha came along, he had dated leggy women without much substance. But then she showed up to the haunted bed and breakfast investigation. Short in stature with curves for days, his heart fluttered the first time he saw her. He spent the whole night talking her ear off and trying to impress her with every bit of trivia he knew. Halfway through the night, he gave up, thinking she had better things to do.

The ghost haunting the place chose that moment to arrive. Aaron dropped the cocky act, becoming all business. Together, they worked to record and document the moment. By then, he spoke to her like he had nothing to prove.

And then the ghost locked them in a room together. It took a while for them to get out, but by then, Aaron knew Tabitha was the one for him. Maybe someday he would try to thank the ghost.

Tabitha insisted she weighed more than she'd like, but Aaron disagreed. To him, she projected perfection. Her blonde hair had been longer when they first started dating and not as colorful. Over the years, she cut, she styled, and she dyed it various colors.

At that moment, she had grown it out from the short, spiky cut she'd had that past summer. It fell long enough to tuck behind her ears, but not much longer. For the winter, she had added purple streaks to it.

But the best part were her eyes. They were a dark, maybe royal blue, and so much intelligence exuded from them. The color lightened or darkened depending on her mood.

His world revolved around her, and he wanted to hang on to that world forever.

"Aaron!"

His attention snapped back to his team when McKenna called his name. She doubled over, one hand flat on her stomach while the other hung on to Tristan's arm for dear life. He ran over to them.

"What happened? Mac, are you okay?" He set the EMF detector on the ground.

McKenna gasped and clutched her stomach. "So much pain," she said through clenched teeth. "Someone is in so much pain."

A glow appeared above the water, dim at first and then brightening. Aaron lifted his head and raised his flashlight. The flashlight blinked once before going dark. McKenna and Tristan's flashlights did the same. Aaron fished out his phone to help him see, but it lost battery life, too. The glow sharpened into the shape of a young woman with long, straight hair that fell to her waist. She wore a sweater and bell-bottom pants. A blue tint surrounded her whole being.

She held out her hands and flew across the water in a span of seconds. She stopped right in front of Aaron. He wanted to check the EMF detector, but his gaze stayed on the ghost. His body froze in place, not one muscle twitching.

Her lips formed a word, but no sound came from them.

"She's terrified. And in so much pain." McKenna forced out the words through gasps.

"Tristan, are you getting anything?"

"Flashes, mostly. Slipping under the dark water and not being able to breathe."

Aaron waited for Tristan to react to the vision, to become the person whose eyes he saw through. Nothing happened. Tristan's dark shape didn't move.

"You're not letting her take you over." It tumbled out as more of an observation than a question.

"I don't know why. It's like there's a barrier between her and me."

"It's the outdoors." McKenna gritted her teeth, still fighting the emotions swirling around inside her. "The energy isn't as strong."

Aaron locked his eyes on the ghost. She hovered in the same spot. "You're Amanda, aren't you? Amanda Perez?"

She merely studied him, her eyes narrowed. She then mouthed more words, her face contorted in a scream. But she still created no sound.

"We want to help you. We want to understand what happened here and what happened to the others that have disappeared." Aaron wished he had grabbed a tape recorder. Sometimes, human ears didn't catch ghostly voices, but recording devices did. He flicked his eyes to Tabitha and her sisters. He didn't need a recorder; they had a medium.

The ghost followed the movement of his eyes. She brightened before whisking across the lake, making a beeline for the sisters.

Aaron pulled out his walkie-talkie and prayed the battery still worked. When Tabitha's voice crackled through, he breathed a little easier.

"She's coming for you."

4

This is so stupid. I'm freezing and nothing is happening." Tabitha wrapped her arms around her body in a futile attempt to ward off the cold. "You only get a few more minutes." She tightened her jaw, hoping her teeth would stop chattering.

"Stop grumbling." Lisa took two steps toward the forest and put her hands on her hips. "I don't understand. It came quicker the last time we did this." She stomped around in a circle.

"Maybe it's not going to happen this time?" Corrie suggested. She hopped in place. "Tabby's right. It's getting colder, and maybe our hands touching had nothing to do with it? Maybe it is random." She pulled out her phone to check the display.

Lisa balled her hands into fists. She paced back and forth like a tiger in a cage. "But this is the same date, the same time. I don't understand." She whirled. "And put that phone away. Noah and Caitlyn are fine."

Corrie pressed her lips together as she tucked her phone away. "It's not a sure thing, Lis. The portal doesn't open like clockwork," she argued. "If it did, everybody would know about it."

Tabitha's walkie-talkie sprang to life. She pulled it out in time to hear Aaron's broken warning. "She's coming for you. Turn around." She whirled in time to see a faint bluish-white glow speed across the water.

She hit Corrie on the padded shoulder. "Incoming!"

Corrie had enough time to gasp before the ghost jumped into her body. Her head slumped for a moment. When she raised it, her blue eyes glowed with fury. Her expression appeared dangerous.

Tabitha took a step back without thinking about it.

"Leave! It's not safe!"

"No!" Lisa jumped in front of her. She glared down at Corrie. "Not this time. Open the portal."

Tabitha tried to pull her back. "If she says we need to go, we should probably listen to her." She waved her hand in Corrie's direction. "She took over Corrie's body before she had time to let her in." She fought the ball of fear growing in her stomach. In all the years she'd seen her sister use her power, she'd never seen a ghost push in like that. How powerful was this ghost? And did they need to mess with her?

Corrie sneered and yelled at them in Spanish. Tabitha barely remembered any of her high school Spanish classes, but the tone clued her in that the ghost told them to leave again. And not in a nice way.

Lisa poked Corrie's chest with her forefinger. "You haven't opened the portal yet."

Tabitha put one hand on Lisa's shoulder and the other on Corrie's and tried to pull them apart. Neither budged. But at that moment, lights danced in a circle next to one of the trees in front of them. Tabitha lifted her head and watched them swirl. Fear crawled up her spine.

"No!" Corrie threw her head back and screamed. "He's coming! It's too late!" The ghost pushed out of Corrie's body. Tabitha caught her sagging sister, stumbling under her weight.

Lisa didn't come to help. Instead, she walked closer to the lights. They continued to dance until they formed a defined circle that grew larger by the minute.

The wind blew harder. Tabitha's feet slid along the crunchy ground as if the circle pulled her toward it. She held onto Corrie. Another gloved hand clamped down on her arm, and she realized Lisa helped along her momentum.

She fought against the portal and her sister. Her heart pounded in her chest as her breath came in short gasps. *Wrong! Wrong! Wrong!* The portal wasn't meant for them. It wasn't meant for anyone. But someone or something wanted them on the other side. Dread settled over Tabitha. For a brief moment, she swore she saw a figure beckoning them. She blinked, and it was gone.

Corrie's eyes fluttered open. She tried to regain her footing, but she couldn't seem to get her balance in the wind. Tabitha attempted to let go of her, but she missed the opportunity.

The portal expanded. Tabitha saw darkness inside. Light hovered on the edges but didn't reach deep down. She wrestled against the pull, jerking her body. Her muscles ached. Lisa pushed her forward, and her feet left the ground. The darkness swallowed her. Aaron screamed her name. The force yanked her away from her sisters. Then she heard no sound at all and saw nothing.

Tabitha tumbled through endless darkness. She twisted and turned, plunging head over heels. She didn't know which way went up or down. She weaved and bobbed. She reached for anything solid to grab, but air passed her outstretched hands.

When she thought she'd fall forever, she landed with a thud on her back. The air left her lungs. An ache spread from her back to her arms and legs. For a moment, she couldn't move. She opened her eyes to see tall, bare trees towering over her. Misty fog surrounded them, giving everything a gray look. A woodsy, damp smell surrounded her as she struggled to sit up. She saw nothing but endless foggy forest. No lake. No moon. No Aaron.

She didn't see her sisters, either. She dusted leaves and dirt off her pants as she climbed to her feet.

Fear crept up her spine. "Lisa! Corrie!" Her voice echoed in the vast nothingness. "Aaron!"

No answer.

What the hell was going on? Where did everyone go? Did she land on the other side of the portal? Was there another side to the portal?

Her body shook, but she didn't feel any cold air. Something cracked, and she flinched. She whirled in the direction the sound came from. No one was there.

Calm down. You have to calm down. She forced her body to stop shaking and took a deep breath. Then another. *Think.* She had to think. She had been next to the lake with Lisa and Corrie. The ghost hopped into Corrie's body, screamed at them to leave, and then left when the dancing lights made a big circle. The portal sucked her and her sisters inside, and she landed in the middle of nowhere.

For the first time, she noticed warmth, not the bone cold of a March night in the Blue Ridge Mountains. She pulled off her gloves and took off her hat. She shoved them into her coat pockets. Tucking her blonde and blue streaked hair behind her ear, she turned around to see the misty forest on all sides.

If she were framing a photo, she'd focus on the spindly trunks of the trees. Concentrate on how the fog curled around them. In photoshop, she'd make the picture black and white. On impulse, she reached for her camera. Her hand met empty air. She lowered to the ground, searching. Her camera meant everything to her. All of her pictures, her way of expressing herself. She pawed the ground and checked behind trees. Nothing. She sat back on her heels, groaning.

"Damn! What an expensive waste."

She dove into the pocket of her coat and retrieved her cell phone. She still had her sisters' numbers programmed in. She turned on the display, and her hopes fell. No connection, no bars. No way of contacting her sisters or home. Swallowing, she stuffed the useless gadget back into her pocket. She stood again, wondering which direction to take.

"Welcome to my world." Tabitha whirled to see the ghost standing next to her. She didn't look like a ghost now. Instead, she seemed solid and in full color. And able to talk. Her voice held a light Spanish accent. Long, straight brown hair fell past her shoulders, and her skin was a deep gold. Sadness filled her dark brown eyes. She wore a tight, green sweater and bell-bottom jeans. She also didn't look as threatening as Tabitha remembered.

"What do you mean, your world?"

"As far as I can tell, this place might be Hell, but I don't know. When I'm not on the lake, I'm here." She frowned. "Now, you're here, too. I'm sorry about that, but I did tell you to leave."

"You did." Tabitha unbuttoned her coat. "What's your name?"

"Amanda. Yours?" Tabitha noted the name. Her guess had been right.

"Tabitha. The two women who came with me are my sisters, Lisa and Corrie. Corrie is the one whose body you hijacked."

Amanda wrapped her arms around her middle. Her dark golden skin seemed to shine. "I'm sorry about that, too."

"You should probably tell her that, but she'd forgive you. If you do it again, though, she likes to be asked." Tabitha shrugged out of her coat. "Speaking of, you don't happen to know where they landed, do you?" She tied the coat around her waist.

Amanda looked around. "They're here. I feel everyone who's here." She closed her eyes for a moment. "I think one is over there." Opening her eyes, she pointed to a cluster of trees to her left. "And the other shouldn't be far behind you." She indicated another cluster past Tabitha. Her eyes unfocused for a moment. "No, she's moving away. I hope to safety."

"Good to know. Have you talked to them like you're talking to me?"

She shook her head. "You seemed to be the safest."

"Ah." Tabitha nodded. "Are we dead?" She wanted to get that question out of the way.

"No. I don't think so." A corner of Amanda's full mouth quirked. "Well, I'm dead, but I think you're still alive. We're just in another realm." Amanda twirled a lock of hair around her finger. Without the blue and ghostly appearance, she manifested as young and innocent as a teenager.

Panic rose in Tabitha's chest. She remembered all of those reports of missing people. People who hadn't returned. Did the portal kidnap them, too? Amanda did say she perceived everyone there. And was she ever going to see Aaron again?

She took a deep breath and tried to remain calm. "Who's everyone?"

"Everyone?"

"You said you could feel everyone who's here. Who's everyone?"

"The people who came through the portal, like you." She looked down. "And the monsters."

"Monsters?" Tabitha's mouth went dry. She backed away from that topic, not wanting to know the answer. "So, which way to the exit?" She steadied her voice, even though she shook inside. *Stay calm. Stay cool*, she thought. Screaming and crying wouldn't help her. It never did.

Amanda shrugged. "I don't know. All I know is once you enter, you can't leave. Once this place has you, it doesn't like to let go."

"But you can come and go."

Another shrug. "I think that's because I'm dead, but again, I don't know."

Tabitha sighed. She declined to give up. Not this early. "There has to be a way out."

"I wish. The portal only sucks things in and doesn't let anything out." Again, Amanda frowned. "I'm sorry."

"You're very apologetic."

Amanda smiled. "I've been told that." Something roared in the distance. Amanda jumped as she dropped her smile and fear crossed her expression. "No, not again. How did he find me so fast?"

Another roar echoed through the fog.

Tabitha stood still, her heart racing. "What is that?"

"A nightmare. Run!" Amanda turned on her heel and took her own advice. She raced away from Tabitha.

Tabitha started after her. "Wait!"

But Amanda disappeared into the fog.

The ground shook as a third, closer roar sounded. Tabitha circled as her breath caught in her throat. A swirl of blackness headed straight for her. Memories of the shadow Drew had fought off in November came back to her. She ran into the trees in the direction she thought Amanda went. She zig-zagged through them as heavy footfalls crashed behind her.

She hid behind a massive tree trunk, trying to make herself as small as possible. She pressed her body against the rough bark as she peeked around it. If the trip through the portal didn't kill her, the monster might.

A huge, black-shaped thing lumbered through the woods. She made out arms, legs, claws, and two glowing red eyes. The black smoke obscured the rest of its features. She whirled back around and put her back against the tree. Behind her, she heard snuffling. The thing sniffed for her. She crouched and huddled against the bark, her heart racing. She tasted bile in the back of her throat.

Thundering crashes reached her tree and stopped. She held her breath, hoping the large, black monster would go away. Minutes ticked by. Her heart pounded so loud she swore the monster could hear it. She pressed her back into the rough bark, wishing she could sink into the tree. After what seemed like forever, the monster passed her, the booms of its steps thumping one after the other. After a while, the sound disappeared.

Eerie silence descended in its place. Tabitha licked her dry lips as she moved away from the tree. As she came around the trunk, she saw no sign of Amanda. She stood alone in the vast, foggy forest.

AARON'S FEET POUNDED AGAINST THE GROUND AS HE RACED around the lake. His heart seized. He watched a large black and white hole suspended in mid-air suck his wife and her sisters into it. He was too far away.

"No! Tabitha!"

It collapsed in on itself with a pop, leaving only Tabitha's camera and the rest of the equipment in its wake.

He reached the spot and turned in a complete circle. She had stood there moments ago. Two minutes had passed since she disappeared into the portal. His ears pounded as his throat dried. How did this happen? Where the hell did Tabitha go? He rounded the nearby trees, expecting her to jump out and yell surprise at any minute. She did not.

The whoosh of a sliding door pulled him out of his red fog. Drew tumbled out of the van, his face white and his eyes rounded in huge circles. "Aaron." He choked out the name.

They locked eyes.

"What did you get?" Aaron rumbled. He stomped to the van.

"Everything, man."

Adrenaline surged. "Go through it frame by frame. Tell me if you see anything that can help us."

"I'm on it." Drew ducked back into the van, the door slamming behind him.

"Aaron, are you okay?" McKenna ran to meet him, Tristan right behind her. Both were out of breath but seemed to be fine.

"No!" he spat. He bunched his fists at his side and yelled. Yanking off his glove, he punched the nearest tree. Pain rattled through his hand, but he didn't care. He hit it again and again until the skin on his knuckles broke. He left spots of blood on the trunk.

His breath rasped in and out of his lungs as he stomped on the cold, hard ground. Why did he let her do this? Why didn't he stop her? Where the hell was she?

Aaron saw McKenna flinch out of the corner of his eye, and he bit back his temper. He didn't want to take his feelings out on her, especially since she already sensed what churned inside of him. Her empathic ability to feel emotions made her one of the best psychics he ever knew, but at that moment, he wished she couldn't feel a thing. He forced himself to calm down and to think rationally. No amount of yelling and punching was going to bring Tabitha back. He cradled his aching hand. "Are you and Tristan still seeing and feeling things?"

"No," they answered simultaneously.

"The pain was gone the minute the portal closed," McKenna said.

"Along with the vision," Tristan added.

"Get in the van," Aaron ordered. "I'll be in there in a minute."

"Are you sure?" McKenna touched his arm. "Do you want me to ease the anger?"

"No. I need to feel this," he snapped. When she jerked back, he softened his voice. "Give me a minute, Mac. Please."

She nodded and dropped her hand. They climbed into the warm van and shut the door.

Aaron yelled into the night. He dropped to his knees as he held his injured hand. He scooped up his neglected glove. His raw throat worked as he held back tears that threatened to fall. He refused to cry in front of his team. He raised his head and studied the dark trees.

"Where did you take her?" he demanded.

The trees didn't answer him. The loneliness weighed heavily in their stony silence.

A tear escaped. He rubbed at his eyes, hoping his team hadn't seen anything. "Okay, portal, open up and give me back my wife." He climbed to his feet as he glared at the trees. "Do you hear me? Open right now." He whirled in a tight circle. "Amanda! I know you're out there! Open the damn portal!"

Nothing happened. The lake remained quiet.

Tabitha was gone, maybe dead. He didn't know if she'd ever come back. According to the reports, no one came back.

He looked at the blood on his fist. He was useless, and he started a fight with a tree. He waved his hand as sharp pain seeped in.

He wanted to strangle Lisa. She'd planned the stupid investigation. She went into it recklessly with no thought for either of her sisters. He'd seen her do this before—her recklessness hurt people and damaged property. He'd be damned if Tabitha was a casualty.

Cradling his injured hand, he kicked the tree again for good measure. His anger waned, not getting him anywhere. Pulling his coat tighter around him, he climbed into the van. Shutting the door, he shed his coat as the heat hit him.

"Feel better?" McKenna asked.

"Much." He kept his eyes on Drew. "What do you have?"

Drew cued the video and hit play. It came from the camera positioned next to the van, pointing out to where the trees met the lake's shore. Tabitha and her sisters stood far away in the left of the frame. Drew fast forwarded through the arguing. He stopped when the lights started to dance.

"Here's where it gets weird." He pressed play again.

The lights swirled around, faster and faster, until they created a huge circle of light-edged darkness on the right of the screen. Aaron leaned closer, watching in horror as an invisible force pulled his wife into the portal. It snapped shut with an audible *pop*.

"Did you see anything that might have caused the portal to open?" Aaron asked as he grabbed the monitor, desperate. "Anything we can replicate?"

"No. Tabitha, Corrie, and Lisa were touching, but that's it." Drew paused the video.

"Maybe there is something to the three theory." Tristan raked a hand through his black curls.

Aaron grunted, releasing the monitor. He pushed down on the fury rising in his chest. "We have to open it again. We have to go after her."

"And then what?" McKenna rested a hand on his arm. "We get sucked in, too, and none of us can get out? That's not a good idea."

Aaron jerked his arm away. "Then what do we do? No one has ever come back from that portal. Read the reports." He drove his fingers into his hair, every nerve in his body zinging. Adrenaline pumped through his veins. He wanted—needed—to do something. "At least I'd be in there with her."

"We'll find something. The ghost is hanging around for a reason. She's in a lot of pain, and I know she's connected to the portal somehow. It seems she only appears when it does. We just have to find out why and how." McKenna pulled open the van door. A whoosh of cold filled the area. "I'm going to grab the equipment. Then we're going to hash out a plan." She hopped out. "You need to bandage your hand."

Aaron watched her leave, blinking in surprise. He grunted as he glanced down at his knuckles again.

"I don't think I've ever heard her talk to you like that," Drew said.

"That makes two of us." Aaron's voice sounded gruff to his own ears. "And I hate that she's right."

"Better go help her, or I'll never hear the end of it." Tristan followed her outside.

"What do you want to do about the Institute van?" Drew jerked a thumb at the black van.

Aaron sighed. "I guess we'll have to call someone to pick it up."

"And what are we going to tell them? That a portal ate Lisa and Corrie, and Lisa had the keys with her?" Drew raised a blondish-brown eyebrow.

"I don't know, Drew. But we can't leave it here. I'll think

of something." He nodded to the lake. "Go help them with the equipment."

Drew nodded and bounced out of the van.

Aaron sat in the quiet for a moment. Were they really going to leave Tabitha here all alone? He considered sleeping out in the cold, but it wouldn't help anyone, least of all him. Cursing, he joined the rest of his team.

5

Tabitha felt like Alice trying to navigate through Wonderland. She expected the spindly trees and dead leaves to start talking to her at any moment. If they did, she hoped they'd tell her where Corrie and Lisa were and how to get out of this Godforsaken place.

She pushed up the sleeves of her sweater. Even though the sun didn't shine, the temperature remained tepid. Well, warmer than the cold night she'd left.

The overgrown and undefined path she followed seemed to zigzag through the forest, but she had no idea where it led. The trees and the fog stretched out forever in all directions.

"Am I even going in the right direction?" Tabitha stopped and turned a full circle. "You know, Amanda, I can use a little help here." She sighed. "I'm talking to myself. That can't be a good sign."

When her voice echoed, she clamped a hand on her mouth. She remembered the monster from earlier, wondering if it might lumber back to finish her. Her stomach twisted as terror spiked. *Smooth move, Tabitha*, she thought. That was all she needed. Death by teeth and claws.

If she died here, would Aaron ever know? Her heart ached when she thought about her husband. What was he doing? Probably trying to open the portal again. She hoped he left it alone. As much as she missed him, she didn't need him stuck in this place with her.

She studied her surroundings. Where did this place even exist? Could anyone find it on a map? Did it stretch beyond the forest, or did it have an end point?

A branch cracked behind her. Pulled from her thoughts, she turned in time to see someone dart behind a tree. "Who's there?"

A high-pitched giggle broke the quiet. Tabitha swallowed.

"Amanda?" she asked, trying to keep her voice steady.

The giggling continued as a little girl peeked from around the tree. Tabitha froze. She knew that little girl, had seen her many times in the mirror growing up. Someone had braided her long, blonde hair into pigtails, and she wore a pink princess dress, her favorite. Tabitha stared at herself at the age of seven.

She stepped back, a chill running down her spine. People didn't go around seeing themselves as children every day. That warning of wrongness echoed in her mind again. She moved back again, creating distance between herself and Young Tabitha.

Young Tabitha didn't say anything. She turned on a heel and ran in the opposite direction. Tabitha knew to leave it alone, but she couldn't stop thinking about her child-self. Maybe it wasn't evil. Maybe it led to the way out. Tabitha took off after her. Her younger self might be a sign that her sisters were nearby.

"Wait! Can you tell me what's going on?" Against her better judgment, she continued to chase the little girl.

Young Tabitha giggled as she deftly avoided trees and branches. She offered no answer as she zipped through at a quick pace. Tabitha didn't remember running that fast at seven. It seemed unnatural.

The little girl burst through a cluster of trees. Tabitha raced after her and barely skidded to a stop at the edge of a cliff. Her child-self balanced precariously on the edge.

"Catch me. Then we can play together forever," she smiled. The little girl danced on the edge, no fear in her wide, blue eyes. She stood on her tip toes, spread her arms out, then jumped backward off the cliff. Her laugh rang through the forest.

"No!" Tabitha rushed forward, her hand outstretched.

Someone caught her other arm before she followed her younger self off the cliff. "Don't!"

The person jerked, and she stumbled back into them. Together, they fell onto the ground in a heap.

Tabitha untangled herself and scrambled to her feet. She struggled to catch her breath from the exercise and the fear. She studied the person who saved her, wondering if the strange world had set another trap.

He looked back, not saying a word.

She swallowed, choosing to do the decent thing. "I'm sorry. Are you hurt?" She offered her hand.

"I'm good. As long as you didn't follow that thing." A young man with dark green eyes and light brown skin clasped his hand in hers. He stood as he shook leaves out of his short, straight, dark brown hair. He towered over her. "It's not safe to follow things through the woods." He brushed dirt off his jeans before adjusting the bow and quiver of arrows on his back.

Tabitha noticed them. She arched an eyebrow at the odd choice in weapon. Who would carry a bow and arrows around? It took a beat for her brain to catch up with his words.

"Thing? That little girl wasn't a thing. She looked like me."

Tabitha dusted dirt and leaves off her jeans and coat. "I don't know how that's possible, but she did."

"It's a *thing*. Best term I can think of to describe them. Whatever they are, they can look like anyone and everyone."

"They?"

His eyes bore into hers. "Your nightmares."

She stopped cleaning her clothes and swallowed. "You mean these woods have more than monsters hiding in them?" The cold fear settled in her gut again. She didn't like the sound of that realization.

"These woods have a lot of things hiding in them."

Tabitha pulled back her shoulders and shoved down her terror as she put on a brave face. She didn't think she should let the stranger know how scared she felt. "How do I know you're not one of them?" She crossed her arms over her chest. "Better yet, how do you know I'm not?" In moments like this, she wished she were taller. At five feet and three inches, she never came off as intimidating.

"All good questions." He jerked a thumb at his chest. "I'm not because I just saved your life. And I don't think you are because you were walking around like you were lost." He nodded at the cliff. "Something like her has a purpose in mind."

"A purpose?"

He arched a dark brow. "To kill you."

"Creepy." Tabitha pressed her lips together. "So, were you spying on me?" She focused on acting angry and indignant instead of giving in to the terror hanging out in her chest. She narrowed her eyes as she tried to channel the haughty tone her mother conveyed when she was mad.

"No. We saw you and two other women come through the portal." He nodded his head in the direction she came. "Every time it opens, we try to get out, but it closes too fast."

Tabitha dropped her arms to her sides and walked away from the cliff, casting a nervous glance back at it. "We?"

"The few of us who are left." He fell into step beside her.

She let the haughtiness go. "Where are the rest of you?" Tabitha searched the woods but didn't see anyone else. She hoped this strange man told the truth and didn't lead her to another trap.

"They found one of the women you were with and are heading back to our campsite. I saw you running this way after the thing and wanted to help." His features softened. He stood tall with broad shoulders. His battered coat and torn jeans looked like they had seen better days. She imagined him in mid-shot with the forest framing him, determination on his face, steel in his eyes.

Tabitha latched on to what he'd said. "You found one of my sisters? Which one?"

He rubbed his chin. "She said her name was Corrie?"

Tabitha let out a breath of relief. Corrie was alive and safe. "Now I just have to find Lisa."

"Lisa is your other sister?" He moved away from the cliff, and Tabitha followed.

"Yeah, my older sister. She's probably intimidating the locals as we speak, but I'd really like to find her." Tabitha bit her bottom lip, glancing away from the stranger.

The stranger chuckled. "She sounds interesting."

Tabitha lifted a corner of her mouth. "Listen for yelling and swearing."

They didn't say anything else as they made their way back to the area where Tabitha landed. She stopped and regarded the sky above the patch of forest. Gray, like the rest of the sky, and it held no indication a portal had been there. Part of her hoped the gateway still hovered above them, but spindly treetops greeted her instead.

"Do you always know when the portal opens?" Tabitha

shoved her hands into the pockets of her jeans, her eyes continuing to scan the trees.

"It makes a hissing noise before it opens. We usually have enough time to get there, but not enough time to get through." He cleared his throat. "I don't even know if it would let us through. I've been trying for months now."

Tabitha lowered her head and met his eyes. "Months?" She tried to ignore the sinking feeling in her stomach. Was she doomed to stalk the portal each time it opened, hoping she got through before it closed?

The man rubbed the back of his neck. "It feels like months, but time doesn't seem to move here."

"What year did you get sucked in?"

"2010." He held up a hand. "And, yeah, I know it's been years. The girl who came through before you told us."

Tabitha perked up. "A girl came through before me?"

"Yeah. Young, about sixteen. Said her name was Monica. She dropped in a couple of hours ago."

"Back in the real world, Monica's been missing for a week." She pressed her back against a tree and let the magnitude of the situation settle in. "Time does move differently here." She blew out a breath as a weight rested on her shoulders. She'd never see Aaron again. She'd never feel his arms around her or hear his deep voice tell her he loved her. Or even if she did get back, he could be an old man.

Damn it! She argued with him the last time she saw him. If she didn't get back to the real world, it would be the final memory he had of her. It would be the last memory she had of him. Her heart ached at the thought.

Tears pricked at the corners of her eyes. Before she knew it, they tracked down her cheeks. She brushed them away. No! She swallowed the rest of them. She was a paranormal investigator, damn it! Born and bred. She refused to cry in front of a stranger. She would find a way out of there.

"You okay?" The man asked.

Tabitha nodded. "I will be." She swallowed, fighting to control her emotions. She took a deep breath and wiped her eyes. She looked up at the young man. "What's your name?"

"Eric Coleman. You?"

"Tabitha Lawson." At least he wasn't a stranger anymore. And she wasn't walking in the woods alone.

Eric started moving again, this time in a direction away from her landing site. "Come on. I'll take you to the campsite."

Tabitha shook her head. "Thank you for the offer, but I have to find my other sister. Lisa is still out there." She started after him, her arms wrapped around her middle.

Eric stopped speaking for a moment. He rocked from one foot to the other as he regarded a spot behind him. After a minute, he dipped his head. "Okay. Let's track back that way. But be careful. A lot of things stalk these woods." He turned around and headed in the direction he watched.

Tabitha pushed away from the tree. She jogged to catch up with him. Eric's long stride ate the distance. She took two steps to his one.

"Can you slow down?" She huffed as she trotted to keep pace. She had no idea how long she'd been walking since she landed.

"Sorry." He eased his quick walk.

"How do you know where you're going?"

Eric shrugged. "Been here a long time. I've gotten to where I can tell the difference between the trees."

Tabitha swallowed. She didn't want to be there that long. She was fine not knowing her way around, even if it meant running into another demon monster or something even worse masquerading as her younger self.

They cut through the brush until they reached the makeshift path. Eric turned left, marching down the winding trail. Tabitha quickened her pace to keep up. They made it halfway down the lane when they heard a roar.

Tabitha froze as her legs shook. Was the demon monster hunting again? Did he haunt this part of the woods? Her mouth went dry as her body tensed. She exchanged a glance with Eric.

His expression was stone. His jaw twitched as he waved a hand, motioning for her to get behind him. She stumbled back a couple of steps.

The ground shook as the black demon monster stalked out of the woods. His roar echoed all around them, deafening them. Tabitha's hair blew back. The monster lifted a hand and swung down to her.

6

Tabby!" Aaron jerked awake. His whole body tensed, ready to fight an unseen enemy.

He blinked a few times, and his office came into focus. Books covered every surface of his desk. He wiped his mouth, still tasting the paper from the book he'd slept on. His computer sat off to the side with a screensaver of a ghost dancing across the monitor.

He yawned and wiped his eyes. He rubbed his aching neck. He probably fell asleep working again, and he hated sleeping at his desk. With a sigh, he dug his phone out from under the pile. He clicked through and brought up Tabitha's name. He thought to tell her he accidently nodded off in the office. When her smiling face appeared on his screen, he remembered the night before.

The investigation. The portal. Tabitha sucked into another world, a place he couldn't follow. All the anger and fear rushed back. He remembered why he fell asleep at his desk.

The team got back to Asheville early in the morning and parked the van at Aaron's house. After everyone headed to their homes, Aaron found he couldn't rest. He climbed into his car and sat in the dark and the quiet. Gripping the wheel, he let the emptiness sink in. She wasn't there. Neither the car nor the house felt right without Tabitha there. For a moment, he thought about driving back to the lake and sleeping underneath the trees where the portal had appeared. If the portal opened again, he could jump in and find her.

But he needed to have a plan to get out. With that on his mind, he started the car and drove downtown. Everything was quiet and still that early in the morning. No one stirred. Even the bars had closed. Aaron felt like he had the whole city to himself.

He replayed the night over and over in his mind. If he had stood with Tabitha and her sisters, he could've stopped her from going in. The portal could have taken him instead. If they had listened to Amanda and run, Tabitha would be with him. He tried to think of various things he could have done in a different way, but no amount of wishful thinking changed the fact that Tabitha remained on the other side of a portal.

When he reached the office, he pulled out every book he had that mentioned portals. He read through nonsense, fake accounts, and scientists asserting their fake facts proved the nonsense, but a couple of the books held kernels of truth. Mostly the information Lisa gave them about a trauma in or near a body of water causing them, how they made psychic powers stronger, and dancing lights appearing were true.

He then hit up a few websites, hoping to dig deeper. Mostly, he came across legends of ghosts and other entities streaming out of portals, but nothing about a portal sucking people in. When he hit the sites about time slips, he knew he had gone too far down the rabbit hole.

Nothing explained where Tabitha and her sisters went or how to free someone from a portal. The Laureline Lake portal seemed to be the opposite of all the information. It didn't want to let anything or anyone go.

Aaron groaned as he checked the clock. Nearly eight in the morning. He had slept there all night. He winced when he noticed the aches in his body. He hated falling sleep on books. He stretched his arms and legs, trying to work out the pain.

He rubbed his neck, stood, and yawned. He had a couple of calls to make: one to the Greene Institute so someone could pick up the van, and one to Noah Parker, Corrie's husband. He owed his brother-in-law the truth.

He called the Institute first. When the secretary answered, he gave her a quick rundown of where the van was located but didn't offer any other details.

He then pushed down his nerves and dialed Noah's cell phone. Noah worked at one of the banks in Charlotte, doing something in finance. Aaron didn't quite understand what his brother-in-law did for a living, but he did know Noah always kept his cell phone on him.

Noah answered after the third ring.

"Hey, Noah." Aaron dropped down into his chair.

"Hey, Aaron. I've got to get to a meeting. What's going on?"

Aaron sighed. "Something bad happened last night. Corrie isn't coming home for a while." He couldn't bring himself to say never, especially when he refused to believe it.

"I noticed Corrie hadn't come home yet this morning, but I figured she was at Lisa's place. What happened?" Worry laced through his tone.

"You know what she was working on, right?" Aaron swallowed. Noah knew what his wife did for a living. The Greenes never kept it a secret.

"Yeah." The jostling sounds on Noah's end stopped.

"She, Lisa, and Tabitha found the portal they were

looking for, and it sucked them in. I'm sorry, man. I couldn't stop it." Aaron wiped his face, guilt beating against his heart.

"What does that mean?" Noah sounded cautious.

Aaron sighed. "It means they're stuck in some other world, and I don't know how to get them out."

Noah stayed quiet for a long moment. Long enough that Aaron thought the call had dropped. "Is there a chance you can get them out?"

Aaron straightened. "There's always a chance. Don't worry. I'm going to find a way to bring her home, man. I'll bring all of them home." He jutted his chin out, even though Noah couldn't see him.

Noah didn't answer right away. The silence made Aaron feel even worse than he already did. Finally, his brother-in-law's soft voice returned. "Is there anything I can do?"

Aaron relaxed his tightened fist. "Not right now, but I'll let you know."

"Okay." Noah took a shaky breath. "Call me as soon as you've found a way."

"You have my word."

He ended the call, his heart heavy. He wanted to crawl under his desk. Calling Noah had been more difficult than he thought, but the man deserved to know why his wife wasn't home yet. If he had left it to the Institute, Noah would never know the truth.

At that moment, he heard keys in the lock at the front door. He swore. Someone entered the office, but he really didn't want to talk to anyone else. The door opened, the bell above it jingling. He opened his door to see McKenna set her bag on her desk. Of course, it would be the empath. The one person who made hiding impossible. She paused and lifted her head.

"Good morning, boss." She turned to face him. "I see you're still pissed."

Aaron grunted. Time for coffee. "I'm always pissed." He stalked past her and headed for the break room. The coffee they bought tasted terrible, but at least caffeine filled it.

"Were you here all night?" McKenna followed him.

Aaron selected a packet of coffee beans and started the process of turning it into warm, brown liquid gold. "Well, you wouldn't let me stay at the lake."

"Too cold to sleep there." McKenna hitched a hip on the counter. "You'd freeze."

"But at least I'd be there in case..." He broke off, not really wanting to voice his thought. Coffee dripped a steady stream into the glass container. He watched as it gained an inch, and then another.

"In case Tabitha came back?" McKenna asked.

"Yeah."

"I hate to say it, Aaron, but I don't think that's how it works."

Aaron raked a hand through his hair. "You're right. It sucks, but you're right." His jaw tightened as he clenched his teeth. He tried to develop an idea, but nothing came to mind. He drummed his fingers on the counter. The coffee dripped forever.

When the pot finished filling, he grabbed the handle and poured some into his black and white mug that read "Ghost Expert" on one side. He didn't miss the irony in those words. The rich, warm smell filled the room. He took a sip, enjoying the dark, strong, if slightly burnt, flavor.

"I guess that's my cue to leave you alone with your coffee." McKenna backed out of the break room.

Cradling his mug, Aaron followed her out. Her last statement ran through his mind. "How it works," rang clearly in his ears. His brain caught up with the conversation.

"How it works," he said out loud.

"What?" McKenna turned around.

"How it works." He repeated it, an inkling of a thought forming.

"Yeah, I heard you the first time."

Aaron set his mug on the edge of her desk. "We need to figure out how the ghost portal works. If we knew why it's there and why it opens, we might be able to figure out how to rescue Tabitha."

"And her sisters, and Monica."

Aaron waved a hand at her. "Yeah, all of them."

McKenna settled on the edge of her desk. "How do we do that?"

"I don't know." Aaron took another sip. "But I'm going to figure it out."

The phone rang, the shrill sound causing McKenna to jump. It echoed in the otherwise quiet office.

"Restless Spirits. This is McKenna. How can I help you?" She listened for a moment before her smile melted away. "One moment, please." She put the other person on hold. "It's for you."

Aaron raised an eyebrow. "Who is it?"

"Philip Greene."

The coffee turned sour in Aaron's stomach. "What does he want?"

"He wants to know where Lisa and Corrie are. They were supposed to check in last night after the investigation."

Aaron pinched the bridge of his nose. Of course, Philip Greene, Tabitha's dad and head of the Greene Institute, would know what Lisa and Corrie were doing. It also probably didn't help that Aaron had called about the van. He clenched his fingers on the handle of his mug. "I'll take it in my office."

"What are you going to say?"

"I have no idea."

With a sigh, Aaron walked into his office and closed the

door. Setting the mug of hot coffee on his desk, he picked up the phone. "Hi, Philip, what can I do for you?" He kept his voice cheerful, even though he hated dealing with his father-in-law and former boss. Keeping everything civil took effort.

"Where are they?" The older man clipped his words.

"Where are who?" Aaron took a sip of coffee and looked out his window. The sun beamed as people walked past, probably heading to open shops and restaurants up and down Haywood Street.

"Don't play dumb with me. I know Lisa planned to go to Laureline Lake and find the ghost there. She told members of her team not to come. She said she'd be back before morning. She's not answering her phone, and she hasn't come home." Philip took a breath. "Our remote viewer can't find her or Corrie."

Aaron shuddered. He was comfortable around most psychic powers, but remote viewing gave him the chills. Just the idea of someone watching his every move from far away gave him the creeps. Tristan once told him that his father, Matthew Johnson, could do something similar but promised that he believed in boundaries.

"I don't know what to tell you, Philip." Another slow sip. "We did see them last night. We hunted for the ghost, got some readings, then everyone went home." Not entirely a lie. He only left out a few details. Extra points for keeping his voice even, especially since the image of Tabitha disappearing into the portal played on repeat in his mind.

"You know something, Lawson. You always do." Philip growled. "What happened? What readings did you get?"

Aaron leaned back in his chair. "I'm not at liberty to say since you aren't a client. But don't worry. I'm sure they'll turn up."

"I'll find out one way or another. I've heard stories of the portal there and the disappearances." He paused. "Did my daughters go into it?" For a moment, it almost sounded like Philip had a heart.

Aaron almost wavered and spilled the whole story. But he stopped himself. He didn't want the Institute involved until he found a way to save Tabitha and her sisters. He dropped his cool demeanor. "If I hear anything, I'll let you know."

"You can start by telling me everything now."

"I need to gather more information." Even though Philip protested, Aaron said good-bye and hung up.

His father-in-law wanted answers, and Philip Greene dug until he learned the truth, at the expense of everyone and everything around him. His determination made him extraordinary and terrifying at his job.

Aaron jiggled the mouse connected to his computer. It woke up, revealing a website he had scouted the night before. The site presented a deep dive into the legend of Laureline Lake. It listed all of the people who had died or vanished there since 1974, including Amanda Perez. The picture of the smiling woman matched that of the ghost he had faced the night before.

"Who are you?" he asked the picture. "And what do you have to do with the portal?"

7

Tabitha stumbled back as the mighty claws whooshed past her. Cold wind followed in their wake. The breeze brushed her hair away from her face.

"What the hell?" Her heart jumped into her throat as her brain tried to interpret what her eyes saw.

The monster swung down again. This time Tabitha didn't move fast enough. A claw scrapped down her arm leaving large, jagged marks. She cried out at the sharp, quick pain as blood oozed out. She clamped a hand over it in an effort to stop the bleeding.

"Get out of the way!" Eric yelled.

She ran for the nearest tree, surprised her legs and feet still worked. Out of the corner of her eye, she saw Eric nock an arrow. He pulled back, his eyes narrowing. When he released it, the arrow flew true and hit the monster in one of its eyes. Its whole form broke apart like a wisp of smoke before reforming a second later. It roared, setting its sights on Eric. It bore down on him.

Tabitha pressed her free hand to the rough tree bark. She

hated cowering and running away, but she had nothing to fight with. What weapon could possibly bring down a monster like that? A sword? A gun? Fairy dust? Her arm stung as she lifted her hand. She watched sticky blood seep through her sweater. She sucked in a breath, replacing her hand. Was a scratch supposed to bleed that much?

Eric dodged the monster's claws as he raced ahead of it. He chose a spot, readied another arrow, and let it fly. This time it struck the monster's chest, dead center. The monster once again broke apart, but instead of reforming, the pieces flew in all directions. Eric turned on his heel and grabbed Tabitha's sticky hand.

"That won't hold him for long. We've got to go." He ran off into the forest, dragging Tabitha behind him.

"What about Lisa?"

"We'll have to wait to look for her. Right now, we need to get out of here."

"No!" She jerked her arm out of his grasp. Her other arm throbbed with pain. "I won't leave without her." Lisa was out there somewhere. What if the monster found her? What if it already had? She didn't have time to dwell on it. She raced away, in the opposite direction, from Eric.

Behind her, she heard him swear, but she didn't stop. Lisa had to be in that neck of the woods. They strode near the landing site. Hopefully, she remained there.

"Lisa!" Tabitha called. "Answer me!"

The throbbing pain in her arm caught her attention. She glanced down at it, a mess of bloody jags bleeding right through her clothes. She gritted her teeth and rolled up her sleeve, careful not to hit the wound. When she reached it, she peeled the fabric away from it with slow, careful movements and sucked in air. Pain shot through her. Tears stung the corners of her eyes.

"Wait." Eric jogged to her. "Wait. Go easy." He meticulously pried the fabric away from the gashes and finished pulling the sleeve up. "Hope this sweater wasn't expensive." He untied Tabitha's coat from around her waist, rolled it up, and wrapped it around her bleeding arm.

"It doesn't matter. It's just a sweater." Her arm still hurt like the devil. "Thank you." She wiped the blood-covered palm of her hand on her jeans but not much of it came off.

"Look, I know you want to find your sister, but these woods are full of things that want to hurt you. We need to get back to safety. You're not in any shape to fight anything else."

She met his eyes. "I can't leave her, Eric. Please."

He sighed. "Okay. Okay."

Together, they trudged through underbrush and around a few large tree trunks until they heard grunts and roars ahead of them. Tabitha stopped short when Eric held out an arm.

"Stay back," he said. "I'll check it out."

"What if it's Lisa?" Tabitha argued.

"Then I'll bring her back."

With that, he moved through more underbrush and disappeared around a large tree.

Tabitha groaned. She hated being useless. She paced, her arms at her sides, as she worked off some of her frustration. She stayed out of the way and waited, stalking the small space. But she needed to know if one of those grunts belonged to Lisa.

Finally, she couldn't take it anymore. She crept through the woods, trying to stay silent. She still heard the grunts and roars up ahead, growing louder as she moved closer.

As Tabitha walked around a large tree trunk, someone burst through a bush and plowed into her. She fell backwards, landing squarely on her back. The pain in her arm spiked. She bit back her scream.

"Tabitha?" Surprise filled the person's voice.

She caught the leather jacket before she saw the face. "Lisa!" Tabitha scrambled to her feet. She embraced her oldest sister as relief flooded in. "I thought we were never going to find you." Lisa was alive and whole.

"I thought I'd lost you." She pulled away as quickly as she had embraced her. "But we've got to run. That thing back there is big, nasty, and not easy to kill." She yanked a hair tie out of her jacket pocket and tossed her hair into a ponytail.

"What did you try to kill it with?" Tabitha asked.

"Rocks. Sticks. Anything I could throw at it. My phone didn't even stop it." She glanced behind her. "I loved that phone."

"We can't leave Eric behind," Tabitha glanced toward the fight.

"Who? The knight is shining armor who helped me get away?" Lisa jerked a thumb in the direction she came from. "I don't think he wants us to stick around."

"He's only out here because of me." Tabitha moved closer to the bushes. "We have to help him." Her arm throbbed, and she still had no weapon, but she couldn't leave Eric alone.

Eric burst through at that moment, breathing heavy and eyes wide. Tabitha stepped out of the way to avoid being hit again.

"Go! Go!" Eric pointed ahead. "The camp site is that way!"

Tabitha turned and ran, trusting Lisa and Eric were right behind her. The faster they got to safety, the faster they could plan their way out. Her feet pounded the dirt-covered ground, and she thought her lungs would burst before she made it. Her heart thudded in her ears. She needed to exercise more, but she'd never admit it to anyone else.

Every tree seemed to look the same. How did Eric know the way? Hopefully, they weren't too far from the clearing. Tabitha lost steam, her pace slowing. She wasn't going to make it.

"Keep going! The monster's still behind us!" Eric yelled.

She needed to rest. Everything hurt. Her injured arm throbbed.

As she burst through the trees, she ran into a clearing. Four faces turned to look at her.

Two of them she recognized immediately.

"Corrie? You found Monica?" The words tumbled out before Tabitha could think about them.

Corrie leaped from the ground. She pulled Tabitha into a hug, squeezing. Tabitha had never been so relieved to see her older sister.

"More like Monica found me." She stepped back and peered around her. "Lisa!" She ran around Tabitha to embrace her other sister.

Monica and the other three people in the clearing jumped to their feet. A tall woman with long, black hair, brown eyes, and tan skin lifted Tabitha's arm. Tabitha winced when she saw the red spots on her jacket.

"You're bleeding," the young woman said.

"Yeah, and it hurts like hell."

The woman let go with a bright smile. "Let's have a look." She gingerly unwrapped the makeshift coat bandage.

"Are you really here to take me home? Your sister said that was the plan." The youngest member of the group, Monica stood at Tabitha's height with an explosion of dark curls and dark brown skin. She matched the picture Tabitha had seen. Monica narrowed her dark brown eyes.

Tabitha sank to the ground. "I hope we can get everyone home." She winced as the other woman peeled the coat away. The fabric wanted to cling to the wound. Tabitha gritted her teeth as the woman worked the fabric free.

"I'm Hannah. Hannah Page," the woman said while examining the scratches. "They're not too deep, so that's good." She turned to the red-haired man who hadn't said anything.

"Devin, grab that cloth in my bag and run to the creek. We'll see if we can clean this." She turned back to Tabitha as Devin grabbed the cloth. He dashed into the trees. "That was Devin James. He's kind of quiet."

Tabitha tried to keep her mind off the pain. "Tabitha Lawson. You met my sister Corrie. The one glowering in the corner is Lisa Greene, my other sister."

Corrie crouched next to Tabitha. "How did this happen?"

"Giant black monster. I didn't move fast enough." Tabitha took a deep breath and told the whole story, from landing inside the portal to the conversation with Amanda, all the way to when the monster slashed her arm and Eric took it out with his bow and arrow to when they finally found Lisa.

Lisa's boots crunched fallen leaves as she wandered around the large open clearing. "Well, now we know what happened to the people who disappeared at Laureline Lake. But I thought more than four people vanished over the years."

Hannah answered. "Some people weren't as lucky as we've been." She wrapped a fresh bandage around Tabitha's arm. "The monsters get them, or they give up hope and wander off."

Lisa completed her circle as she walked into Tabitha's line of sight. "Monsters? Like the ones we ran into?"

"Yeah, and it seems like more and more keep coming, and in different forms." Eric met Lisa in front of the nearest tree. "I don't know if we can hold them all back, but this place seems to help."

"Is that all there is here?" Corrie asked. "Monsters and imaginary people that lead you over a cliff?"

Eric sat down, his back to a tree. He grabbed the bag Hannah had indicated and pulled out a pack of blueberries. He offered some to Tabitha and her sisters. "No, there's the strange girl that comes to the edge of the clearing. The one that looks like the ghost from the lake. She won't walk into the clearing, though." He popped a blueberry into his mouth. "And I've never seen her hurt anyone."

"That's Amanda." Tabitha accepted a blueberry. "Have you tried talking to her?"

"She runs away anytime we get near her," Hannah said. "It's pretty amazing she talked to you."

"Where did the bag and the blueberries come from?" Lisa asked as she finally joined everyone on the ground.

Hannah smiled. "The bag is mine. I had it on me when I went through. I tend to carry a lot of stuff. The blueberries we found wandering through this place. No animals, but there's some edible vegetation." Her smile disappeared. "It's starting to become scarce, though."

At that moment, Devin returned with the wet cloth. Hannah took it and went to work. The minute it touched her skin, Tabitha hissed. Tears sprang to her eyes from the sting.

Tabitha listened as her sisters continued to question Eric, Hannah, and Devin. Devin described hearing a strange voice call his name, but the others never heard it. Tabitha shivered.

Eric haled from High Point, a small city near Winston-Salem. At twenty-one, he planned to be the first in his family to graduate from college. His degree concentrated on math, but he was still thinking about what to do with it. Getting stuck in the portal put his plans on hold, though. Eric's bow, quiver, and arrows came with him. He shot on his college team and practiced while camping at the lake alone. The lake provided the quiet he liked. He told them he had clutched his bow and arrows when the portal opened. Fascinated, he had inched toward it, and the portal yanked him through.

Hannah said that her two friends had dared her to venture to the lake. The legend drew them, and they wanted to see it for themselves. She worked as a nurse and always came over prepared. She brought more bags than anyone else on the trip. She thanked her lucky stars she held the bag with the food and the first aid kit when she went through the portal.

"Why did you go near the portal?" Corrie asked.

Hannah shrugged. "The colors, mostly. They called to me." She wrinkled her nose. "Kind of weird, huh?"

Devin told them how he and some friends were creating a documentary about the lake's story when he was pulled in. He wanted to enter the film into local festivals, maybe use it to jump start his career. But in the end, the voice proved irresistible.

"The voice?" Tabitha raised an eyebrow.

"You haven't heard it yet?" Devin shivered. "I hope you don't."

Tabitha wondered how many others followed similar stories. Like Lisa, their curiosity overcame common sense. But they all paddled in the same boat.

By the end of everyone's story, Hannah had bandaged Tabitha's arm with material she carried in her bag.

"Well, we appreciate your hospitality." Corrie stood.

"Yeah, thank you." Tabitha cradled her arm as she got to her feet. "But we have to get out of here."

"There's no way out." Hannah put away the leftover material. "We've looked since I got here."

"She's right," Eric said. "You're stuck here with us. You're welcome to stay. For some reason, the monsters don't come near here."

"Thank you," Corrie said as she stood next to Tabitha. "But I have a daughter I have to get back to."

"I'm sorry." Eric ducked his head. "That portal doesn't stay open for long, and we haven't found another way out."

The sense of dread that started as a tiny ball bloomed through Tabitha's entire body. She dropped her head into her hands and groaned. "We can't just give up! We can't!" She raked her hair back. Exhaustion swept over her. The lack of sleep caught up to her, and she weaved.

"Okay. It was the middle of the night when we came through the portal." Corrie rubbed Tabitha's back. "I say we take some time and get some sleep. Then we'll come at this fresh."

"I could use some sleep," Lisa declared.

"We'll keep watch," Eric offered. "Then we'll switch."

Tabitha didn't argue. She hoped everything looked better after a few hours of sleep.

8

This is our priority now." Aaron placed print outs of Amanda's picture and a still of the portal side by side in the center of the coffee table. "Based on the photo and the timing of her death, Amanda Perez is probably our ghost." He leaned on the table. "What is her connection to the portal? And if we help her, can we help Tabitha and her sisters get out of the portal?"

"How do you know the portal didn't come first?" Drew picked up Amanda's picture and studied it.

"Based on accounts of the area, the portal didn't appear until after Amanda died." Aaron rapped his knuckles on the table. "From what I can find, portals are so rare that most paranormal investigators don't believe they're real. They appear near bodies of water and after a traumatic death."

"Amanda drowned." Tristan tapped the end of his pen on the table. "She screamed and begged, terrified. I won't forget those images any time soon." He shuddered.

Aaron nodded. "Did you see if someone pushed her or contributed to her death in any way?"

"No. It flashed by, and then it was gone. That doesn't

mean it didn't happen." He scrunched his nose. "I'd have to be near her again or have something that belonged to her to try to see a longer vision."

"I think we should split up," McKenna suggested. "You and I can find out more about Amanda while Drew and Tristan research the portal."

"Maybe it'll help to look into the other missing people," Drew set the picture back on the table. He drummed his fingers on the edge. "Find out exactly what they were doing and when they disappeared. If they were sucked into the portal like Monica's friend said, then that might give us a clue on how to get them out."

Aaron pressed his lips together. His team provided solid suggestions, and he trusted his team to take the initiative and find answers. He had started building his current crew a year and seven months earlier, so he knew what talents each person brought to the table. They'd help him save Tabitha.

He felt calmer at the thought that they had his back. He wanted Tristan to see Amanda's whole death and try to find clues, but he knew how swiftly a vision could take his friend. If Tristan lost control, other bits of the past fought their way through him. He refused to put the other man through that.

He dropped into the empty chair next to McKenna. "Are you up for a trip to the Greene Institute? I'd like to see their file on the portal."

A slow smile crept across her face. "And maybe see if anybody is hiding any more information?"

"Exactly." Aaron enjoyed the perks of having an empath on his team, especially if she spent her time reading someone else.

Tristan stood. "Come on, Drew. Let's see if my grandpa wrote anything about portals in his journal."

Aaron thrust a sheet of paper into Tristan's hand. "Here's

a list of some of the people who disappeared. That might help, too."

The two-hour drive to the outskirts of Charlotte didn't seem so bad. While McKenna chattered on, trying to distract him, Aaron ignored the nervousness building inside of him. He hadn't been back to the Greene Institute of Paranormal Research since he and Tabitha left it almost two years before. He didn't trust Philip Greene nor any of the people who worked for him, but if Lisa and Corrie were pursuing the Laureline Lake portal, then they had to have some information already in their files. He'd do anything to give him a better idea about the ghost and the portal.

The Green Institute rose out of the valley as Aaron's car crested the hill.

McKenna gave a low whistle. "I didn't know it was that big. How can they afford this?"

"Greene money and powerful donors," Aaron gripped the steering wheel, his knuckles turning white.

The place was comprised of two stark, gray buildings, one standing in front of the other. To the random passerby, it looked like a warehouse or a factory. But if they took the long road through tall trees and approached the main building, visitors saw the sign prominently displayed on the front in large, green letters. Tabitha's grandfather, Stephen, had suggested the green letters. Green for Greene, he used to say.

Aaron felt the familiar twist of his stomach as they approached the main building. He'd hoped he would never have to go inside again...never face those stark white walls, or the cold, impersonal space. It had the feel of a place where power and information mattered more than people.

A receptionist smiled at them from the front desk, but it still didn't warm the large, open room.

"Can I help you?" she asked. Aaron figured Philip hired

the woman recently because she didn't recognize him. Receptionists didn't last long at the Institute.

McKenna gave the receptionist her brightest smile as she reached the desk. "Hi, Renee." Of course, McKenna noticed the woman's nameplate on the desk. Aaron liked her people skills; she dealt with them better than he did. "We'd like to see Philip Greene, please."

Renee narrowed her hazel eyes. "Do you have an appointment?"

Aaron leaned on the desk and answered before McKenna. "No, but I'm his son-in-law. Tell him Aaron Lawson needs to talk to him."

Renee lifted one perfectly sculpted light brown eyebrow. She tossed her long, brown curls over one shoulder. She stared at Aaron for a long time as if she were trying to figure out if he were lying to her or not. She pressed her lips into a disapproving straight line, picked up her phone, and pressed a button. "Sorry to disturb you, Mr. Greene, but an Aaron Lawson and his bubbly friend are here to see you." She waited a moment. "Yes, sir, I'll send them on back." She placed the receiver onto the cradle. "Do you know how to get to his office?"

"I think I remember the way." Aaron motioned to McKenna and made a left. Family pictures lined the walls of the long hallway that led to Philip's office. Generations of Greenes either smiled or glared stoically at them as they passed.

"Is that baby Tabitha?" McKenna stepped closer to one of the pictures farther down the wall. "She looks so innocent and blonde. I don't think I've ever seen her hair that long."

Aaron sighed, an ache in his chest. "I think she was nine when that picture was taken."

She stood next to her mother, prim and proper in a fancy purple dress with ruffles. Definitely not Tabitha's choice, he'd bet. Her parents sat in the center of the photograph with Lisa standing behind them, a tough-looking fifteen-year old, and Corrie, at twelve, standing next to her father, the only one smiling.

"I never thought about what her life was like growing up in this business." McKenna stepped back. "I probably should have."

"It's all she's ever known." No wonder she wanted to do something else. The last argument they had before she disappeared came back to him. He mentally kicked himself for it. Why didn't he ask her what she wanted? Why did he assume she'd fall into line with his dream? He felt like an idiot. And now she was gone. If she had never joined Restless Spirits, she would still be there, and he wouldn't be standing in the main building of the Greene Institute preparing to talk to his father-in-law.

Maybe he didn't deserve to save her.

McKenna studied him. "You're beating yourself up again."

"Mac."

She shrugged. "Sorry. You were projecting."

"Mums the word on the whole empathic thing, okay?" As they reached the end of the hall, Aaron grabbed the door.

"I promise to keep it under wraps."

Satisfied he'd hid his friend's gift from Philip's prying eyes, Aaron opened the door.

Philip lifted his head and nodded. "Aaron, it's been a while. Have a seat."

Aaron refused Philip's offer. He preferred to stand when facing his former boss and current father-in-law. He still hadn't planned out how to tell the man his daughters were missing without mentioning the portal. He felt the whole situation stayed on a need-to-know basis. And Philip didn't need to know.

For the first time in a long time, he wished he had a

cigarette. Just something to take the edge off. But he promised Tabitha he'd quit, and he hadn't touched a cigarette in five months.

McKenna sat in the chair facing Philip's desk. She presented the picture of innocence as she introduced herself.

Philip sat forward and rested his elbows on his massive, polished, dark-cherry wood desk. "I assume you're here to tell me where my daughters are." He steepled his fingers under his bulky chin.

Philip gave off an air of confidence and intimidation. Every brown and white hair on his head was brushed into place. He always wore a dress shirt and tie, not a wrinkle in sight. He was a large man with broad shoulders who filled the space of every room he entered. He expected people to jump when he asked them to, and he didn't tolerate what he considered deserters well.

He'd stopped speaking to Tabitha when she and Aaron left.

Aaron swore the temperature in the room dropped a couple of degrees as they stared at each other. For a brief moment, Aaron wanted to tell Philip all of his secrets – the portal, McKenna's power, everything. He struggled to keep his mouth closed.

He once admired Philip Greene, but that time had passed long ago.

"Actually," McKenna piped up before Aaron could answer. "We're hoping you can help us solve the mystery."

"The mystery?" He raised a gray eyebrow, intrigued.

"The mystery of what happened to them." Aaron wondered if he should be worried at how well McKenna lied.

Philip leaned back in his plush, brown leather chair. It squeaked as he moved. His sharp royal blue eyes – Tabitha's eyes – regarded them both. Aaron felt like they bore a hole into his head. He knew that look. That look meant that

Philip didn't buy McKenna's story. Aaron fought to keep his expression neutral.

"And how, exactly, can I help you?" he asked.

"We'd like all of the information Lisa had on this case. Everything about Laureline Lake and its ghost." Aaron moved closer to the desk.

"Sit down, Aaron. You don't have to tower over me." Philip snapped to attention, straightening in his chair.

"I'm fine standing, sir." He forced the words through clenched teeth.

McKenna sighed and fidgeted in her seat. "You know, Aaron. It probably won't hurt if you sit down."

Aaron groaned inside his own head. He didn't have time to play Philip's power game. Tabitha existed out there, stuck in another world, on the other side of a portal. Begrudgingly, he lowered himself onto the chair next to McKenna, but he kept his arms crossed.

"Now, information, was it?" Philip asked, his voice pleasant. He leaned forward, a twinkle in his eye. "I imagine you'd like information on the portal as well?"

9

"Tabby?"

She faced Aaron, love blooming in her heart. He rose on one arm, resting at the elbow. His brown eyes sparkled in the low candlelight. She counted the freckles on his bare shoulders.

"Aaron?"

He caressed her face. His soft touch trailed down her neck along her chest and down to her stomach. Chills ran along her skin. She cupped his face in her hands, pulling him closer to her. She pressed her lips to his, parting them enough to let him in.

Her heart beat to the rhythm of the kiss. Slow and sensuous, she savored the taste. She soared with passion, wanting the moment to last forever.

He moved away from her mouth, his lips touching her chin, her neck, and her chest. She trembled as he licked one of her bare nipples. It tickled, and she gasped.

"Oh, Aaron..."

"Tabitha."

Tabitha's eyes snapped open to see dull, grayish light illuminating the woods. For a brief moment, she thought she and Aaron were snuggling in a sleeping bag beside the lake. She reached across the grass, and her hand met empty air. Then she remembered she lay on the hard, dirty ground, not a sleeping bag nor a tent. She curled into a ball with her head resting on her coat. The loss was unbearable. She trembled as the cold and the loneliness set in.

"Tabitha."

She rose, wincing against aching muscles. She wondered where that ghostly voice came from. Aaron's voice sounded deeper, not light and airy. Everyone else but Devin slept, various snores disrupting the silence. He strolled around the clearing with a spear at the ready, not paying any attention to her.

"Hey, Devin?"

He jumped and whirled. "Oh, hey." He rubbed the back of his neck, a blush rising in his pale, freckled cheeks.

Tabitha held out her hands as she struggled to her feet. "Sorry," she whispered. "I didn't mean to freak you out."

Devin pushed back his floppy hair and shrugged. "It's okay."

"Did you call me?" She crossed the clearing, her whole body aching and stiff.

"No." His eyes widened. "Did you hear the voice? Ignore it. It's bad news."

"I remember." She held out her hand. Wide awake, she regarded the rest of the sleeping party. "I can take watch now if you want to sleep."

He gave her a grateful smile and handed her the roughly-made spear he carried. The group had a collection of them that Eric made with a pocketknife, and he'd explained how to use them to the newcomers before everyone fell asleep.

Devin nodded to her arm. "You sure you're okay?"

"Yeah, I'm good."

He nodded again before heading over to the camp site.

Tabitha studied the spear. She'd never used one before, but it looked self-explanatory. If nothing else, she could try to hit something hard. Clutching the rough wood in her hand, she walked the perimeter. No birds chirped, and no other animals howled or croaked. It gave her the creeps.

As she rounded the curve, her eye caught something big and blue through the trees. She recognized a familiar sky-blue color, stark against the gray. She hadn't noticed it when she glanced in that direction before. She stepped out of the clearing, past a few trees, and almost dropped the spear.

Home. Her childhood home. Here, in the middle of this strange forest.

The large, blue Victorian didn't belong there, but it stood among the trees and underbrush, nonetheless. Tabitha veered toward it without even thinking about it. She glanced over her shoulder at her sleeping sisters, wondering whether she should wake them or not. She peered back at the structure. One peek wouldn't hurt. Eric said the clearing remained safe, and she still intended to keep an eye out. Nothing made a sound nor sneaked along the perimeter, so she resolved to check the house out for a few minutes.

Tabitha tiptoed up the creaking, wooden porch stairs. The white porch resembled the one she remembered, right down to her mother's potted plants. Large, brown, wooden rocking chairs lined the space with a matching wooden sidetable between them. She recalled rocking in them when she needed quiet time to think during the summer. Without thinking, she pushed open the front door and stumbled inside.

Tabitha had always thought the large Victorian pretentious. In the real world, it rested on a corner in Charlotte's historical Fourth Ward district. The house originally belonged to her great-grandparents, and they passed it down from Greene to Greene. Her parents occupied it in the present. Since her father wasn't speaking to her, she imagined she wouldn't be next on the list to own it.

Her mother loved the too-large house and filled it with all the fancy furniture and antiques she could find. Tabitha remembered Maria Greene scolding her when she sat on a couch that she shouldn't touch or even thought about going near a lamp. Growing up, she tried not to touch anything in the Greene house. Most of the time, she lost that battle, especially if her sisters chased her or dared her. Broken pieces littered her childhood.

She gasped when she entered the foyer. Every piece of furniture and her mother's prized antiques, including every knick-knack, duplicated the ones in the real world. A handmade bench set against the left wall, shoes underneath it. Through a doorway to her right, a set of Queen Anne chairs and a matching couch rested in the sitting room, immaculate as ever. Ugly lamps littered the first floor. It made her feel as if she'd grown up in a museum.

As she crept further inside, she fought the urge to take off her shoes. Shoes scuffed the original hardwood floors, and Philip Greene wouldn't have that. According to him, those floors cost a fortune to restore and maintain.

But something about the house unnerved her, so her eyes strained to see in the dim light. Her footsteps popped like gunshots on the hardwood floor as something creaked behind her. Then the front door slammed. She pivoted back to it, her hand gripping her spear. She wrapped the fingers of her free hand around the doorknob and twisted. The door didn't open. It didn't even budge. Setting aside the spear, she pulled with all her strength, and it still remained shut. She rattled, turned, and yanked to no avail.

Her hands shook as she released the doorknob. Her heart pounded in her ears. She gulped in air with short, quick bursts. She stumbled back from the door and wrapped her arms around herself. A way out. She needed a way out.

The enormity of her situation crashed over her. She was never getting out. She would die or vanish like all the others. No one knew where she was. Her sisters would never find her. She pressed her back against the nearest wall and closed her eyes.

"Okay, don't panic." She breathed in and let it out in a slow trail. She did it again and again, until her whole body calmed down. Other doors and windows filled the giant house. She would find one that opened. She steeled herself and opened her eyes.

Her eyes landed on the nearest window. "If the door won't open, maybe the window will." She ran to it, unlocked the latches, and pulled. She grunted with effort. Her arms shook. It didn't budge, either.

Tabitha swallowed. *No!* She wiped the sweat from her brow. Her breath hitched. She picked up the spear and held it out in front of her. It bobbled in her slick hands. She prepared for whatever this house threw at her.

"Tabitha Evelyn Greene, you get back to bed. It's way past your bedtime." Maria Greene's thick, refined, South Carolina Lowcountry accent rang through the foyer.

"Mom?" Tabitha jumped but held onto her spear. She pivoted and found herself face to face with a woman she hadn't seen in a couple of years, even though she did make a point to talk to her on the phone when she had a free weekend.

"Of course, it's me." She looked immaculate in a black dinner dress and her blonde hair piled high on her head. Her hair was free of grays and her face of any fine lines. Diamond earrings dangled from her ears. "Now, get back to bed."

"Mom, how do I get out of here?"

Maria's face softened. "Of course. You had a bad dream." She crossed the foyer and held out her hand. "Come here."

She tentatively reached out with her free hand but hesitated. The woman spoke and acted like her mother. However, the wrongness returned. Tabitha knew she wasn't in Charlotte, and she wasn't a child. Also, her mother appeared younger, like she was when Tabitha was little. She remembered she had landed in a portal where people emerged as something else.

"I don't think so."

Maria cocked her head to the side. "Don't be silly. Your father and I have an important event to get to. You need to be in bed." She took a step toward Tabitha.

Tabitha moved back, placing the spear between her and her mother. "You're not my mother."

"Tabitha." Maria pressed her lips together. "You're not playing right."

Maria's form changed. She grew taller and broader, and her hair shifted from a blonde updo to short brown and white. Her father stood before her, his blue eyes glaring.

Tabitha pointed the spear at him. "Stay away from me."

"You never did learn discipline. You never fit in." Philip curled his hands into fists. "You're nothing but a useless extra child. We didn't need or want you."

Tabitha swallowed. She didn't like hearing her own fears echoed back to her, but she refused to believe them in that moment. Sweat dripped down her back as she moved farther away. The panic she experienced earlier threatened to return.

Philip snarled and changed right before her eyes again. He became even taller and thinner. The hair went from brown and white to black, the skin became paler, and black eyes peered at her. Instead of her prim and proper mother or her broad-shouldered father, a handsome, ethereal man stood in front of her. He wore an immaculate black suit.

Terror filled every pore of Tabitha's body as she recoiled. "This isn't real," she said. "It isn't real." She lowered the spear and ran for the door. She whirled, keeping her eyes on the strange man. He didn't move. Her hand fumbled behind her until she felt the smooth brass of the front door's knob. She tried to turn it, but it still didn't twist.

"You're not like the others," he said, his voice deep and silky.

She shook at the sound of it. Her heart pounded in her chest as every ounce of calm she worked for disappeared. Her throat clogged, and tears threatened behind her eyes. She was going to die. She was going to die in a replication of her childhood home, and no one would ever know what happened to her. She'd be another person who wandered off.

She'd be damned if she went down without a fight. She struggled to find her voice. "Who are you?" Tabitha mustered her courage and held up the spear, the pointy end directed at the man.

The stranger sniffed the air. "You don't seem so sure, so pure." His mouth parted into a smile to show gleaming, white teeth. "There's a darkness to you."

Weird and ominous, she thought. Tabitha's hand shook, but she strove to hold it steady. She straightened her shoulders. "Who are you?" Her voice sounded stronger.

"I'm everything you're afraid of." He took a step toward her. "And your fear is delicious." His hand whipped out and caressed her cheek. His touch felt like ice.

She tried to swallow that fear, but it bubbled inside of her. She jerked away as she gripped the spear with both hands, her knuckles turning white.

His eyes widened and gleamed. "Let's play." With that, he disappeared into smoke.

Tabitha didn't waste any time. She ran for the back door. She pushed through the door at the end of the foyer and raced through the kitchen. She tried all the doors and windows, but nothing opened. The house trapped her from all sides.

No! No! No! The tears threatened again, but she shoved them down. Her throat burned with the effort.

She turned down the hallway that led to her father's study and froze.

The monster filled every available space. She had never seen anything so massive. Two beady yellow eyes regarded her. A vague, human-shaped face, complete with a nose and a mouth, appeared. But, when he smiled, she saw rows of sharp teeth stuffing his wide mouth. Nasty, huge, sharp teeth. His large form tensed.

Her heart stuttered as she struggled to breathe. Every fiber in her body told her to run. Her knees went to water, and the spear shook in her hand.

"Come here, little one." The monster's voice rumbled like a truck's engine when it revved. Tabitha felt it down through her bones.

In that moment, she chose to listen to her gut. She turned, still clutching the spear, and ran.

Aaron jerked back and blinked a couple of times. He needed a moment to let his father-in-law's words sink in. Lisa had said her father didn't know anything about the portal. But of course, Philip did. His hand curled into a fist, and for that moment, he wanted to punch Philip. If the man knew about the portal already, then why wasn't he being more forthcoming? Aaron fought to keep his features stoic, but the smile on Philip's face told him he failed.

Philip picked up his desk phone and hit a button. "Davis, bring me the file on Laureline Lake, please." He then hung up without thanking the person on the other end.

"You don't have it online?" McKenna asked. Aaron glanced at her. How could she sit there and stay calm?

Philip waved at the desktop computer. "I've never really trusted those things. Lisa and her team swear by them, but paper is still the best method. Harder to break into and steal." He threaded his hands behind his head. "So, how is my wayward daughter? We missed you at Christmas."

Small talk. Philip wanted Aaron to lower his guard. Aaron

raised an eyebrow. "She's fine. We're fine. Sorry about that. I promised my parents we'd see them for Christmas." He spat the small talk out through his clenched teeth. They didn't have time for pleasantries.

Philip nodded. "I see. Your little ghost hunting business is gaining quite a bit of traction up in Asheville. I heard about The White Lady, and an employee mentioned he heard you broke the curse on a fiddle? Impressive. A big step up from dead pets."

"We're doing pretty well for ourselves." In fact, they had gained a few more clients since Drew defeated the shadow ghost that tried to kill him. According to Drew, Jaime proclaimed her satisfaction with their work by word of mouth and online. Now, more and more clients asked for their help. But Aaron gave the same amount of attention to the woman who insisted she saw her deceased dog laying by her bed as he did The White Lady and Drew's curse.

Davis chose that moment to arrive with a thick manila envelope. She was a thin, pale woman with thick, red hair pinned into a bun and a sharp business suit. Holding her head high, she didn't say a word as she passed Aaron and placed the file on Philip's desk. But as she turned, she lowered her glasses, giving McKenna an assessing glare.

She narrowed her light green eyes.

"Leigh Anne Davis, this is my son-in-law Aaron Lawson and his associate McKenna Ellison."

Davis gave them each a quick nod but returned her eyes to McKenna. She adjusted her glasses as she pressed her lips together.

"Do I have something on my face?" McKenna wiped the side of her mouth and shuffled in her chair.

Davis gave her a slow smile. She continued to stare for a few moments more as she played with the small locket she wore around her neck. "No, not at all." She walked away from the desk and around McKenna's chair. "Your glow is so…interesting."

"My what?" McKenna followed Leigh Anne's progress.

"Your glow. It's so bright, and the colors change so quickly."

"Do they?" Philip asked.

"They do." She focused her attention on her boss as she tucked an escaped strand of hair behind her ear. "Do you want me to tell you everything I see?"

"Not at the moment, Davis. You've already been more than helpful." Philip nodded.

"I'd like to know what you see." McKenna stared back at Leigh Anne, her gaze never wavering. Aaron wondered if McKenna was trying to read Leigh Anne's emotions, and he wanted to know what she learned. The tension in the room thickened between the two women.

Leigh Anne looked away first and straightened her shoulders. "Will that be all, sir?"

"Yes, Davis. You may go."

She turned on a sharp high heel and left the room, the door closing with a decisive click behind her.

"You'll have to forgive her. Davis doesn't have the best social skills, but she is one of the best psychics I have." Philip flipped the envelope open and removed its contents.

"Psychics?" Aaron asked. "I thought most of them jumped ship."

"We still have a few." Philip fanned out the papers on his desk.

"What can she do?" Aaron noticed McKenna's voice shook a little as she angled back toward the desk.

Philip's eyes brightened. "She's a rare one. She sees auras and can actually detect psychic abilities in others. It's curious that she took an interest in you, Miss Ellison." He rested his hands palms down on the papers. Delight filled his features.

McKenna's laugh sounded a little too high-pitched. "That is weird, isn't it?"

"You know, my father worked with a psychic named Lauren McKenna." Philip tapped his chin. "If I remember correctly, she was an empath. A good one." He leaned across the desk. "It can't be a coincidence your parents named you McKenna, can it? Any relation?"

Aaron exchanged a glance with McKenna. She bit her bottom lip and rubbed her hands against her jeans. He had wanted to keep her power a secret, but if Davis sensed the empathy, then it probably wasn't worth it anymore. He gave her a nod, hoping she knew the choice to reveal the truth belonged to her.

McKenna sighed. "She's my grandma."

Philip lifted his eyebrows. "Oh, are you an empath, too?"

Aaron shifted to the edge of his seat. "I think we should focus on the contents of that envelope. We're supposed to be helping Tabitha and her sisters, right?"

"Of course, of course." Philip pointed to McKenna. "But I'd love to talk more about your family."

Aaron tried to send her a feeling that conveyed he had her back no matter what happened. She didn't have to be afraid of Philip Greene. She seemed to visibly calm down. "Maybe some other time," she said.

Philip shrugged. "I look forward to it."

Aaron picked up a newspaper clipping. Amanda smiled at him from the picture on the right. The picture on the left, however, showed officers pulling her body from the lake. "Amanda Perez drowned on March 20, 1974. Officers didn't suspect foul play and ruled it a tragedy." He looked up. "If that's so, then why is she haunting the lake?"

"That's a good question, and one we haven't been able to answer." Philip slid a page of typed words across the desk. "But the true mystery is the portal. Someone spotted it a year after Amanda's death. We haven't been able to find anything earlier than that. This is a list of all of the sightings of the ghost and the portal, even some of the disappearances." He sat back.

McKenna skimmed the page. "Isn't this the same list you have, Aaron?" She passed it to him.

Aaron studied it. "You're right." He gave the sheet back to McKenna. He reached for the whole folder, knowing it held the information he needed. Philip covered it with his hand, moving it out of reach. A muscle in Aaron's jaw twitched.

"Now, come on, Philip. If we're going to work together, we have to see everything." He kept his tone friendly.

Philip sighed. "Everything?"

Aaron exchanged a glance with McKenna. "Well, if you'd like to lose another team to the portal..."

"I'll give you the information on one condition. You share any new information you learn about the portal with me." He held out his hand. "Is that a deal?"

Aaron rubbed his clammy hands on his jeans. He knew better than to make a deal with Philip. Who knew what the man would do with that information? But he needed the research the Institute already had. He shook Philip's hand. "It's a deal."

Philip stayed silent for a moment. "My daughters went through that portal, didn't they?"

"We don't know..." McKenna began.

Philip cut her off. "I know you, Lawson. You'd want to go with Tabitha. You'd have been at that lake with her, Lisa, and Corrie. They went through that portal, didn't they?"

Aaron deflated as he exchanged another look with McKenna. The whole meeting finished falling apart. "Yeah. Yeah, they did."

Realizing they weren't going to get Philip's full cooperation unless he spilled the beans, Aaron told him everything about that night. He described the ghost and how she took over Corrie's body to warn them. He filled his father-in-law in on every detail of the portal, of how it opened and how it sucked Tabitha and her sisters into it. All he left out were McKenna's and Tristan's psychic reactions to the portal.

"I see." Philip slid the whole file across the table. "I'd like this brought back in crisp condition. And don't forget our deal."

With a promise to keep him in the loop, Aaron took the file. With their business concluded, Aaron and McKenna left.

"If you keep grinding your teeth like that, you'll wear them down to stumps," McKenna said, breaking the heavy silence that had settled in the car.

"I'll be fine," Aaron grumbled.

"Oh, yeah. I can feel your fantastic mood all the way over here." Aaron saw McKenna tilt her head out of the corner of his eye. Some days he hated having an empath on his staff.

"I always feel like I need a shower every time I have to talk to him." Aaron gripped the steering wheel, his eyes focused on the road that led away from the Institute.

"I can understand why. He keeps a lot of emotions guarded, and his shields are excellent for a man with no psychic ability. But he was worried about Lisa, Corrie, and Tabitha. He let that slip for a second before closing up again."

"I don't believe that man has a heart, much less the ability to care."

"He did, a least for that one small moment in time." McKenna paused. "So, anything else on your mind?"

Aaron grunted as he turned onto the highway, relieved he was heading home.

"Okay." Instead of waiting for an answer, McKenna opened the file.

"What does it say about the portal?" Aaron asked, changing the subject.

"Lisa, Tabitha, and Corrie weren't the first team sent to the Laureline Lake portal. The Institute has been studying it steadily since 1975. Philip joined the second team to look into it." The paper rattled in her hand. "I see a lot of numbers measuring the energy output, but I don't understand them. Some of the psychics on the various teams reported being able to control their powers better, and their visions were stronger. No detailed reports about those vision, though. One investigator said the portal felt evil, but they didn't go into detail."

Aaron pressed his lips together. He glanced over at McKenna. "What about the people who disappeared? Were any of them ever found?"

McKenna flipped through the papers until she found the information. "Including Monica, ten people have gone missing at Laureline Lake. Well, now thirteen, counting Tabitha and her sisters." McKenna went quiet.

"What is it?"

"There's a pattern to the dates. The first person disappeared in 1975. Two more in 1980. Another in 1985. Then 1990. 1995."

Aaron picked up the thread. "2000. 2010. 2015. And now. Every five years." He held out a hand. "Can I see those numbers?" She passed the sheet to him. Though their meaning eluded him, he noted the number of disappearances rose in a year ending in zero or five. He handed the paper back to her. "Well, shit. Lisa was right. It is predictable." He tapped his hands on the wheel. "Anything that might connect Amanda to the portal?"

"From what I can tell, she only appears right before it opens. Some years there's no sighting of her at all."

"But every fifth year, there is." He rumbled again. No matter which way they turned, they kept running into a wall. "Have any of those people who went missing come back?" If he had one, just one, who had come back through the portal, he'd have a way to get Tabitha back.

More silence as McKenna looked through the file. "No. Not in the Institute's notes."

"Dammit!" Aaron smacked the wheel. He glared at the road as if it had personally offended him. "We've got nothing! Nothing!"

"Don't give up yet. Tabitha knows the paranormal. She grew up around it. If anyone can get out of that portal, she can."

Aaron glanced away from the road and glared at McKenna. "You're saying I'm supposed to sit around and hope for the best?"

"No, but I think you should trust Tabitha. You do tend to roll over her sometimes."

"That's ridiculous! Tabitha always calls me out on my bullshit. Always." Aaron turned his attention back to the road as he drove around a slower car.

"Not in front of a client. Nor do you let her take the lead."

"Not true. I share responsibility." Aaron clenched his jaw. "I think we need to focus on saving my wife." He gripped the steering wheel so hard his fingers ached.

"Okay. You're the boss."

But McKenna's words rattled around in Aaron's head. Rolling over Tabitha? What did that even mean? He never let her take the lead on an investigation? Yesterday, she said she didn't even want to hunt ghosts anymore. She wanted to take pictures of landscapes and waterfalls for a magazine. She wanted to leave the business they built together and do something that didn't include him.

And that's when McKenna's words made sense. Investigating the paranormal linked him with Tabitha. Had he ever asked her once about her photography? He knew she loved it, and she captured amazing photos. But had he ever really supported her when it came to it? He realized he did roll over her and assumed that she loved investigating as much as he did.

Inside, he cringed as McKenna's point drove home, but he absolutely refused to admit it.

Tabitha raced up the back stairs. She ran down the hallway, past the bedrooms, not daring to glance back. Lumbering footsteps echoed behind her as the monster pounded the floors, zipping faster than someone his size should be able to.

Her breath came hard and quick as her heart thundered. Her muscles ached. *Boom! Boom! Boom!* He closed the distance between them. In all the time she had investigated haunted houses, apartments, and beds and breakfasts, no ghost had ever chased her personally. She'd been knocked aside and caught in the crosshairs, but never the intended target. She didn't like the feeling. She charged down the main staircase and spilled into the foyer, spear still clutched in her hand.

The house shook as the monster descended the stairs.

Tabitha ran for the front door. She checked the lock before trying to open it, but it stayed firmly shut like before. Why wouldn't the stupid door open? She glanced over her shoulder, knowing the monster was coming.

Boom! Boom! Boom! The monster stormed into the foyer, blocking off the back exit. The doors on either side of her that led to other rooms snapped shut on their own. He'd cornered her.

"Come here, little one. It won't hurt a bit," he crooned, his voice deep and creaky. He smiled, showing off all his pointed teeth.

Tabitha wanted to believe the monster lived in her imagination, but she remembered the scars on her arm from the encounter with the forest monster. She tightened her hold on the spear and backed into the corner. She saw no way out. Why did she come into this house? Why did she follow the voice? The others told her not to listen to it. No one knew where to find her. More importantly, no one guarded the clearing. She worried she'd left the rest of the group vulnerable, put everyone else in danger, and that no one would arrive to rescue her.

Tabitha's mouth went dry as her stomach roiled. She glanced down at the spear. She tightened her fingers around it. She could fight her way out. And she declined to go down without one. She'd never used a spear before, but she hoped she learned fast. She raised the spear over her head.

"Come and get me."

The monster rushed toward her at an unnatural speed. Tabitha charged. She shoved the spear through his chest. He stumbled to the side. She yanked her weapon out, took the opportunity, and raced past him. She ran through the dining room and into the kitchen.

The monster roared. The house rattled as he chased her. Plates and cups crashed on the floor.

She studied the spear and saw that no blood covered the tip. Nothing of the monster lingered.

She turned in time to see the monster dive for her. She raised the spear again and stabbed with all of her might. The tip slammed into his chest. This time, she hit dead center, like Eric's arrow had on the last monster. He fell to the side and landed in a heap on the floor. Then he burst into dust, scattering across the air. She let the spear clatter to the parquet floor.

Tabitha sucked in air, adrenaline running through her. Her arms ached as she picked up the spear and ran to the front door. The strange man from earlier stood in front of it. When she saw him, she raised her spear.

This game sucked. She didn't want to play anymore.

"Move."

The man cocked his head as one corner of his mouth turned up. "Intriguing." He departed in a wisp of smoke.

Tabitha reached for the door. The moment her fingers curled around the knob, it swung open. She stumbled into Lisa, knocking her to the ground, and they both tumbled before landing in a heap. The spear fell out of her grip, rolling a few paces away.

"Lisa?" Tabitha scrambled off her big sister.

"Tabby, thank God you're okay." Lisa stood and brushed off her jeans. Then she pulled Tabitha into a hug. "Don't ever run off on your own like that again. You scared the crap out of me."

Stunned, Tabitha hugged her back. "I won't do that again. I promise."

Lisa let go and took in the front porch they stood on. "Damn. This really does look like our house."

"It looks like that inside, too."

Lisa shivered. "We should go."

"Yeah." With one last look at the house, she collected the spear and followed Lisa off the porch.

"How did you find me?"

Lisa shrugged. "I couldn't sleep. When I saw you left, and no one watched the clearing, I got up." She nodded toward the way they came. "When I saw the house, I put two and two together."

As they passed into the trees, Tabitha saw movement out of the corner of her eye. She turned her head in time to see Amanda duck behind a tree and disappear.

"What's going on?" Lisa stopped.

Tabitha pointed to the far trees. "I just saw Amanda. She knows more than she told me. I wonder why she won't help us."

"I don't know." Lisa started walking again. "But there's more going on in that head of yours."

Tabitha's adrenaline wore off. Worry and fear tumbled around inside of her. It all crowded into her head. When she looked at Lisa, the jumbled mess found a target. "We're stuck here, aren't we?" Heat bubbled to the surface. "We're stuck here because you wanted to see what was on the other side of that damned portal." With no fear left, Tabitha let the anger and frustration come at full force.

"We're not stuck." Lisa stopped. She laid a hand on Tabitha's arm. "We'll find a way out."

"Will we?" Tabitha yanked her arm away. "The others have been here for a long time, and they haven't found a way out yet. And what about the people who were killed or wandered off?" Tabitha locked a death grip around her spear. "Ask them if we'll ever see the real world again."

Lisa smirked. "But they didn't grow up around paranormal stuff like we did. We'll figure this out. We always do."

"And what if we don't this time? Are you prepared to spend forever in that clearing? Hannah's almost out of granola bars and bottled water. None of the rest of us have supplies." The anxiety clawed its way up to her throat.

Lisa moved closer until her nose almost touched Tabitha's. "We'll think of something." Her voice rose. "What about Amanda. You said you think she knows more than she's saying. Let's track her down and make her talk."

"Threats and force are the only ways you know how to

solve a problem, aren't they?" Tabitha whirled on her heel and almost ran into Corrie.

"Hey! Your voices are going to attract that monster again. Keep it down and get back to the clearing." Corrie's jaw twitched.

"But she..." Tabitha started.

"I don't care. Go!"

Even though Corrie's voice never rose, Tabitha found herself obeying the order. She turned away from the house and headed into the woods, her sisters behind her.

The three of them walked in silence until they reached the clearing.

Tabitha waved the rest of the group away. "I need a minute." She stalked off to the other side of the clearing and sat down. She set the spear next to her.

The gray forest went for miles and miles. Nothing but trees and fog as far as the eye could see. Was this the only view she'd ever see for the rest of her life?

Her father would have enjoyed every moment of it. A pocket dimension where a person never aged and maybe never died unless a horrible monster or their own nightmares got them? She thought he'd love it. Tabitha pictured him setting up equipment and trying to run tests on the monsters.

But she hated it. What was the point of a place where she never aged without Aaron? She pulled her knees to her chest and stared at the trees. Why did she have that stupid fight with him? He probably still wanted to yell at her. If only she had some way to contact him. To let him know she survived and that she loved him.

Tabitha closed her eyes. She imagined Aaron, framing him like one of her portraits. His hands tucked into his jeans, a knowing smirk on his handsome face, and his brown eyes twinkling. Most people saw Aaron as tough and intimidating, but Tabitha knew the sweet side of him. The side that teased and played. Her favorite side. She ached for him.

She missed him so much. She had to find a way out.

She sighed, sinking into the depths of despair. If she believed Eric and the others, she'd spend the rest of her life in this dimension, dodging monsters and fighting for her life.

T hank you for agreeing to meet with me." Aaron
sipped the warm herbal tea Leah Rodriguez had
given him. "And thank you for the tea."

"No trouble at all." Leah sat down across from him, a soft
smile on her lips. "It's not every day a paranormal investigator wants to come by and talk about my sister."

Aaron set the cup down on the coffee table in front of
them. "I have to admit, I'm surprised. Usually when I say I'm
a paranormal investigator, most people won't open the door."

Leah let out a musical laugh. "Well, I'm not most people. I
believe there are things in this world we can't understand."
She drank from her own cup before wrapping her hands
around it. "I'm probably one of the few people in this world
who has seen her dead sister's ghost."

After not getting far with the Institute's file, Aaron spent
the next two days tracking down Amanda's family. Both of
her parents had passed a couple of years before, and her two
younger brothers had moved out of state. Then he struck
gold with Leah, Amanda's older sister. Leah continued to live
in the area near Laureline Lake with her husband of forty

years. A beautiful woman in her mid-sixties, she fussed with her short, black and gray-streaked hair while her bright, brown eyes regarded Aaron. Her flawless tawny skin bore a few wrinkles here and there. She wore a dark purple sweatshirt and jeans, bucking against any old lady stereotypes Aaron might have had.

Since she invited him to visit and talk for a while, Aaron didn't have to think twice about taking the chance.

The Rodriguezes lived in a two-story brick house off the Blue Ridge Parkway. Trees and a view of Mt. Mitchell skirted the area. Leah told him she hated the drive down into Asheville to take her kids to school and to go to work. The long grocery run continued to bother her. But the view and the quiet more than made up for it. She never liked crowds or noise that much.

Aaron sat in a large, soft armchair that almost swallowed him whole. He imagined settling back in it and resting his feet after a long day. Leah perched on the edge of a matching fluffy chair next to him.

Leah set her cup of tea down, sat back, and crossed her legs. "So, how can I help you?"

Aaron took a moment to get his thoughts in order. McKenna and Tabitha were the ones who usually did the interviews. He did it every once in a while but not enough to know where to begin. He thought about bringing McKenna, but he wanted to speak with Leah on his own to compare her observations with the other interviews in the file. He sipped his tea before he began.

"What was Amanda like?"

Leah's soft smile grew bigger. "Oh, wonderful. A dreamer, really. She believed in the good in people and the world." She paused for a moment as she reached for a nearby picture on the side table next to her. "People like to make their deceased relatives sound better than they were, but I'm telling the truth about Amanda." She passed the picture to Aaron.

He held an old photograph of two young women posing and laughing together. Aaron recognized Amanda right away and figured Leah was the one standing next to her.

"Amanda was an amazing artist. She loved painting landscapes, and she drew the lake most of the time. She said she always felt safe there, like someone watched over her." Leah shivered. "I disagreed. Something there felt wrong to me." She wrapped her arms around herself.

Aaron passed the picture back. "Wrong?"

"Wrong. I agreed that someone watched us but stalking us rather than protecting us. I didn't buy into my sister's optimism. I felt cold and exposed when I was there." She made a sign of the cross as she spoke.

Aaron thought about that. "I didn't feel anything at the lake."

"It's changed since Amanda died. It bothers me, but no one watches me." Leah sighed. "It's hard to explain."

"No, I understand what you're saying." Aaron made a mental note to ask McKenna if she felt anything about the area. "You don't have to explain."

"Anyway, Amanda loved with her whole heart. If she loved you, she'd do anything for you, no matter what."

"If I may ask, how did she die?"

Leah's smile faded. "An accident. My parents didn't want to believe that, but it was. I told her not to go to the lake at night, but she never listened to me. She insisted she liked to spend her time roaming and thinking by herself." She settled back into the seat. "The night Amanda died, she fought with her boyfriend right on our front porch. He broke up with her, and she cried.

"I tried to talk to her, to help her through it. But she argued with me. She kept saying how the whole thing was her fault. She took the car and headed for the lake." She paused and looked down at the floor for a moment.

"It's okay. Take your time." Aaron wrapped his hands around the still-warm teacup and waited. In his own experience, he also found it hard to discuss the dead.

Leah dabbed her eyes before she lifted them and continued. "I saw her body when they pulled it from the lake. Not a mark on her. It looked like she slept." She sighed. "Amanda never learned to swim. She must have slipped and fallen into the water. She drowned."

"Did the police say whether someone else was there or not?" Aaron kept his voice low and steady.

"They didn't find evidence of foul play. For a while..." Leah trailed off as her voice hitched. "I'm sorry. More than forty years later, and it still breaks my heart."

Aaron looked around the room. He realized he didn't have any tissue on him. He mentally kicked himself for not thinking to bring any. Still, he remained quiet.

Leah excused herself for a moment. She rushed to the nearby powder room. After a couple of minutes, she returned more composed with a tissue in her hand. She apologized again as she returned to her seat.

"You're fine," Aaron said. "I didn't mean to upset you." He wished he knew of a better way to comfort her. McKenna and Tabitha were so much better with people than he was.

Leah waved him off. "I knew where this conversation would lead, and I still said yes." She dabbed at her eyes. "Now." She took a deep breath. "The police tried to rule it a suicide, but I know my sister. She was upset, but she wouldn't have killed herself."

Aaron nodded. "I only ask because of the nature of ghosts."

"The nature of ghosts?"

"It's not an exact science, but most ghosts hang around

because they have unfinished business. They're searching for something. Many of them want to see their killers brought to justice." *Please don't think I'm crazy*, Aaron thought.

Instead of tossing him out of her house, Leah seemed to consider the idea. "It makes sense. Why else wouldn't they move on?"

"The case of your sister is a strange one. Not only do we not know why she's still here, but she seems to guard a portal that appeared after she died."

Leah's face went stark white. "The portal? You've seen the portal?" She dropped her hands into her lap.

"Yeah." Aaron moved to the edge of his seat. "You know about the portal?"

Leah crossed herself once more. "That portal is evil. Pure evil. I saw it the night I saw my sister. The night she warned me away from it. I heard a voice inside of it calling my name."

Aaron tried to hide his surprise. Out of all the accounts he read, not one of them mentioned a voice calling their names. Even Tabitha had never mentioned it. "Can you describe the voice?"

"Dark, deep, soft. It actually lured me to the portal. But then my sister appeared like an angel. The moment I saw her, the voice faded."

"You didn't see her before it appeared?"

Leah rubbed her hands on her jeans. "I did. You see, my husband and I went up there because of the legend. Because of the description of the ghost. We arrived in March 1980, right before our wedding. I waited for five years because I wasn't sure I wanted to know. But Guillermo talked me into it. We drove over and waited for it to get dark.

"Then I saw her, walking along the edge of the lake. She looked up, and I swear she saw me. I think she recognized me. Then the portal opened, and the voice. But somehow, Amanda kept Guillermo and me away from it. And then she and the portal disappeared. It was the strangest experience of my life."

"Do you know who the voice belonged to?" He leaned closer.

"No." Leah shook her head. "It could've been the devil for all I know, but I don't ever want to know. It was evil. Pure evil."

H ow are you?"

Tabitha lifted her head to see Corrie standing next to her. She knew it wouldn't take long for her middle sister to check on her.

Tabitha wiped her eyes. "Better. Not as cranky." She blinked. "How are you?"

"Sad. Hurt." Tears shined in Corrie's eyes as she sat down. "I miss Noah and Caitlyn so much. They don't know where I am, Tabby. At least Aaron knows you're here." Drops tracked their way down Corrie's face. "Noah and Caitlyn won't even know what happened to me." Her breath seized on a sob. "Oh, God. Caitlyn's going to think I abandoned her."

Tabitha wrapped her arms around Corrie. "No. No, she's not. If I know Aaron, he'll make sure Noah and Caitlyn know where you are." Her heart broke for Corrie, for her little niece. A niece she hadn't spent a whole lot of time with and regretted every moment she'd missed.

They let a comfortable silence fall between them. Corrie wiped away her tears while Tabitha held her. Footsteps came closer to their small huddle, and Lisa sat down in front of them.

"Look, I'm sorry." She rubbed the back of her neck while she offered the apology, but it sounded sincere. "I was so focused on learning more about the portal that I didn't even think about how we'd get out. Tabby, you were right. This is my fault." She raked a hand through her long hair. She pulled one knee to her chest, wrapping her hands around it.

She sighed as she narrowed her eyes. "I'm going to find a way out of here. I'm not giving up." She held her sisters' hands. "You both have always been important to me, and you don't deserve spending the rest of your life here."

Tabitha let go of her anger. "Neither do you." She knew Lisa. Her sister wanted to see how things worked, whether mechanical or paranormal. She spent most of her childhood tearing things apart and fixing them like new. It made her a lousy sister sometimes but a good paranormal investigator. She built state of the art tech, things other investigators coveted. But she worked so hard at it that she forgot about the people around her.

Tabitha took a deep breath. "Too bad you can't build something to get us out of here."

Lisa released her sisters. She drew her other knee to her chest. "It doesn't matter if I can build something. I'll figure something out."

"You still think we can get out of here?" Corrie wiped her red, tear-stained face. "Eric, Hannah, and Devin have been here for a long time, and none of them have found a way out."

"None of them grew up around the paranormal," Lisa pointed out.

"True," Tabitha agreed. She glanced behind her to see the other four huddled together. Her gaze landed on Monica.

She hadn't given up like the others, and Tabitha couldn't give up on her. She turned her attention back to her sisters.

"Have you learned anything else from the others?" she asked.

Lisa shrugged. "Not much. They go out in pairs to hunt for food. Hannah's granola bars are starting to run low. If anyone hears the sound of the portal, they run through the forest to see if they can catch it. Apparently, it doesn't open in the same place twice so Eric hasn't been able to predict it yet."

"But doesn't it open in the general area?" Tabitha asked.

Lisa's brow wrinkled. "I think so, but it still doesn't stay open long enough for anyone to try to get out."

"What about the other people who came through? Hannah said some of them wandered off. Maybe they found a way out in the opposite direction?" Corrie suggested.

"I haven't asked about that." Lisa rubbed her chin. "That's a good question." She nudged Corrie with her foot. "Now you're thinking like a Greene. Dad has a whole bunch of faults, but he always said that 'Greenes can....'"

"...always come up with a solution,'" Corrie finished. "I know the quote well."

Listening to her sisters talk things through, Tabitha's anxiety eased. She thought about searching for a way out. She recalled the walk through the house, and the strange man who met her there.

"A monster wasn't the only thing in the house," she blurted.

Her sisters stopped chatting.

"What do you mean?" Lisa asked.

Tabitha told them about seeing their mother turn into a strange, lean man. A man who told her she was different than the others and had a darkness to her. Corrie shivered while Lisa kept still.

"But he didn't try to kill you?" Corrie asked.

"No. He told the monster to."

Lisa pressed her lips together before jumping to her feet. She motioned to Tabitha and Corrie to follow her. "Hey, Eric! Got a question for you."

Eric stopped packing his quiver with new arrows made from sticks he'd collected. He sighed as he gave Lisa his full attention. "What?"

"What do you know about a strange dude stalking around here siccing monsters on people?"

Hannah and Devin both froze. Monica merely looked confused. Eric seemed to mull over the question, his expression thoughtful.

"You saw him?" Devin moved closer to them. He swallowed.

"Him?" Monica's brows dipped down.

"You mentioned the voice to me. Is the strange man the one calling our names?" Tabitha directed her question to Devin. "Who is he?"

Devin lowered his eyes. "I don't know. But yeah, he calls my name sometimes." He met her eyes, his wide with fear. He gripped her uninjured arm. "You listened, didn't you? I told you not to." His voice rose on every word.

"Whoa! Whoa!" Eric held out his hands as he stood. "I've been here longer than you. No one's ever called my name."

"I've never heard mine either," Hannah said. "Like Devin, I've been here since 2015."

"But I bet others have. That's probably why they wandered off, like I did." Tabitha raked both hands through her hair, trying to think. "It's not just random monsters and images stalking this place. Something intelligent is out there, and it chooses some people but not others. Why?"

"Maybe it's Amanda?" Lisa offered.

Tabitha brushed off her jeans. "Maybe, but she didn't

strike me as the sinister type." She bit her bottom lip. "Then again, The White Lady in Tristan's apartment didn't kill anyone when she lived. Her anger and confusion drove her revenge. She killed men who resembled the ones she blamed for her death."

Monica jumped to her feet. "Are you telling me something is stalking us?" She whirled on Eric. "I want to go home now!" She stuck out her chin, glaring at the taller man.

Eric groaned. "There is no way home." Defeat weighed heavy in his tone.

Tabitha put her hands on her hips. "You seem sure of that. You're not listening to any options."

"There are no options. Stay here or become monster food. You've seen what's out there. This is our reality. Permanently."

Lisa stepped into his personal space, her hands curled into fists at her sides. "How long did you look? Did you check every corner?"

Eric glared down at her, his eyes flashing. "I've nearly died too many times to count. I'm too busy trying to stay alive." He gestured to the group. "I'm trying to keep all of you alive." His jaw twitched.

Lisa opened her mouth to argue, but Corrie beat her to it. Corrie jumped to her feet, marching over to him. She poked his chest with each word. "I can't accept that, Eric. I have a little girl back home who needs me. I can't stay here!"

Tabitha widened her eyes in surprise. People perceived Corrie as the quiet sister, the peacemaker. She rarely ever raised her voice. But when it came to her family, her temper flared.

Tabitha turned to Devin. "Tell me what happened when you saw the strange man."

Devin rubbed the back of his neck. "I heard him call my

name, like you did. I followed it to a place that looked like my house."

"The place you grew up in?"

"Yeah. He said darkness lived in me, too."

"Did he tell a monster to kill you?"

Devin nodded. "Yeah. I fought my way out, but barely."

Tabitha tucked a strand of hair behind her ear. "Maybe he's testing us."

"Why?"

"I don't know."

"You heard that!" Lisa's voice got louder. "Something is targeting my little sister. We have to get out of here now."

"Eric's right. There's no way out of here." Hannah stood next to Eric, her arms crossed over her chest. "We can't go home."

"Did you even try?" Monica joined Lisa's side.

"Did you miss the part where several people tried and never came back?" Hannah asked.

Tabitha took in the stalemate. Her side clearly had more people, but Eric's side had more experience. Hannah's words rattled around in her head.

"Wait. If those people never came back, how do you know they didn't find a way out?" she asked.

Eric crossed his arms over his broad chest. "Because I found their bodies."

"All of them?" Lisa asked.

He shuffled from foot to foot. "No, but I found enough of them."

"Are their spirits still here?" Corrie asked.

"I don't know."

"Could Amanda sense them?" She continued to press.

"I said I don't know."

"If they did find a way out, they wouldn't leave us, would they?" Hannah hugged herself, her brow creased.

"Nobody found a way out. This place killed them." Eric stood firm, the muscle in his jaw twitching.

"I think we're getting carried away here." Tension filled the air, and Tabitha did her best to diffuse it. Arguing made the problem worse. "We need to know everything you know about this place. We need to work together."

"And what's out there in the real world for me?" Eric tossed his hands into the air. "It's been ten years. My girl-friend probably married someone else and had their kids." He tapped his chest with his fingertips. "I missed part of my life, and my entire family probably thinks I'm dead."

Hannah and Devin nodded in agreement.

Devin pressed his back to the nearest tree. "My friends and I came to the lake on a dare in 2015. A stupid, stupid dare. Five years ago." He raked a hand through his floppy red hair. "My friends have moved on."

"It's the same for me." Hannah rubbed Devin's left shoulder.

"I'm sorry." Tabitha reached out. "I am. But we can't hide here forever. If something intelligent is in this world, it'll figure out how to get into the clearing at some point. We've got to..."

She didn't finish the sentence. The ground shook beneath her feet. Everything rumbled. She heard something snap in the distance. Everyone dropped to the ground and covered their heads.

"How often does this happen?" Tabitha struggled to yell over the crashing and rumbling.

"Never!" Eric said. "I've never seen this." Tabitha strained to hear him over the noise.

That didn't sound good at all. A creaking sound drew Tabitha's gaze to the trees. A large crack split down the middle of one. Another creak, and the tree came apart. Half of it started to fall, heading straight for Lisa.

Her heart in her throat, Tabitha dove for her sister. She and Lisa fell to the ground right as the tree hit the spot where Lisa had been lying.

As quick as it started, the shaking stopped. Everything went quiet.

Tabitha moved her arms and lifted her head. Other than the half of the tree, the clearing remained the same. But around it, many of the trees in the forest rested on the ground.

She struggled to sit up, adrenaline pumping through her veins. Two arms wrapped around her and pulled her into a tight hug.

"Oh, God! Tabby." Lisa crushed her. "Thank you."

Tabitha returned the hug, trying to remember the last time she and Lisa had shared so many in one stretch. "It's okay. Are you hurt?"

"No, you?"

Tabitha finally freed herself and checked. "I think I'm okay." She turned to the rest of the group. "Everyone okay?"

"I'm good!" Eric called.

"We're okay over here." Corrie and Monica were on their knees.

"Devin? Hannah?" Tabitha yelled.

"Here! We're here!" Some fallen branches moved. Hannah crawled out with Devin following. Both shook dust and dirt from their hair. "We're not hurt."

Tabitha stood, her knees quaking. She helped Lisa to her feet before making her way across the clearing.

"Does anyone know what happened?" Monica asked, her dark eyes huge.

Lisa dusted off her jacket. "No, but I bet this clearing isn't going to be safe anymore."

14

A aron rolled over and reached across the bed. His hand landed on the empty space next to him. His hand brushed cold air. He grabbed the edge of Tabitha's pillow and breathed in her scent. It still held the faint smell of vanilla from her shampoo. He sat up, pulling the soft pillow into his lap, and cradled it. Rocking back and forth, his heart ached from how much he missed her.

He dragged himself from the bed, showered, and dressed. Silence encompassed the car as he drove to work without Tabitha. He realized when he did get her back, his drives might continue to be this quiet. She had made it clear she wanted to try for that new job instead of being a full-time investigator. Could he get used to that?

He pushed the thought away. *One problem at a time.*

The talk with Amanda's sister Leah gave him a clearer picture of the girl behind the ghost. But he wondered what to do about it. Her version of events matched the copy of the police report in the Institute files. Everyone called Amanda's death an accident. Then what business did she need to finish? Aaron tapped his fingers on the steering wheel as he pulled into the parking garage. And how did it connect to the portal?

And then he learned the new information about the strange voice. Another ghost? Something else? Aaron heard of other, darker things lurking in haunted places. Things that weren't human. But he was jumping to conclusions, right?

Respectable investigators ignored the stories about evil, dark entities searching for a foothold into the world. They ventured further into fiction for his taste. He kept the thought in mind, but he didn't want to pursue it without further proof.

He pushed those thoughts away. His goal centered on bringing Tabitha home. After a week without her, life lacked meaning and joy. He found himself going through the motions, unable to concentrate on the other cases that needed his attention.

McKenna greeted him when he walked through the front door, the bell tingling overhead. She wasn't alone. Tristan stood at her desk along with an older version of Tristan. A tall, portly man with gray hair and green eyes laughed, slapping his son on the back. His skin appeared lighter than Tristan's, but the features were unmistakable. The man rubbed his salt and peppered beard as he held out a hand. His joy and friendly manner lightened the room.

"Matthew Johnson." No wasted words or small talk. Aaron approved.

Aaron shook the offered hand. "Aaron Lawson. Can I ask what you're doing here, sir?"

"He's here to help." Tristan raked his curls out of his eyes.

Aaron lifted a brow. "How?"

One of the doors at the back of the room opened, and Drew walked out. He carried his laptop with him. "Oh, good. You're all here."

"What's going on?" He knew he had taken the day before

to visit Leah, but he expected someone to keep him in the loop.

Drew continued to the meeting room. "You told us to research the portal, so we did."

"I checked Grandpa's journals. He hadn't dealt with the portal before, but my dad has," Tristan said.

Matthew eyes brightened. "Imagine my surprise when he mentioned Laureline Lake. One of my cases connected to that place."

"And the laptop?" Aaron pointed to Drew's haul.

Drew patted his precious machine. "Found a video on YouTube of the portal. It caught something our cameras didn't."

Aaron turned his attention to McKenna. "Did you know about this?"

"Yesterday while you were out."

"And you didn't tell me."

She beamed. "Tristan was so excited. He wanted to tell you himself."

Tristan rolled his eyes. "What am I? Five?"

Aaron raised his eyebrows. He knew his team consisted of the best people and that bringing Tristan in after The White Lady added to it, but they impressed him. He rubbed the back of his neck. "What about the other clients you scheduled today?"

McKenna tapped the keys on her computer keyboard and studied the monitor. "Mr. and Mrs. Reyes will be in at eleven. Mr. Scott will be in at two. Then we have the results for the Granville house to deliver at four."

Aaron winced. He had forgotten about the Granvilles. "I haven't even compiled..." he started.

"Already done." McKenna smiled at him. "That's what you pay me for."

"Okay." Aaron sighed. "Let's see what you've got." He gestured toward the meeting room.

Drew set his laptop at the head of the oval-shaped wooden table. He found the site and prepared the video. He hooked the whole thing to a projector as everyone grabbed a seat. Aaron settled in a seat to the left of Drew and peered around the room. He missed Tabitha's relaxed presence. When a wave of melancholy washed over him, a hand rested on his.

"We're going to get her back," McKenna said.

"Mac."

She rolled her eyes. "You're projecting. I can't help it." She dipped her head. "Want me to take some of the worry away?"

Aaron shook his head. "Feels a bit like cheating."

"Just let me know, then." She let go and sat back.

Aaron pulled his shoulders back, trying to give off an air of confidence. Being the head of this organization, he would damn well take the lead. "Okay, Johnson, what did you find out?"

Tristan hopped out of his seat, turned on the projector, and centered the picture in the middle of the wall. Drew stood next to him. They looked like a couple of middle schoolers preparing to give a report. Tristan cleared his throat, clicked a few keys on the laptop in front of him, and clicked the remote for the projector. A PowerPoint presentation appeared on the wall. Aaron rolled his eyes.

"Drew and I went through a lot of stuff looking for any mention of the Laureline Lake portal and other portals in general." Tristan hit the space bar. A picture of a portal popped up. Bullet points swooshed in from the left. "As you know, a portal is..."

"Johnson." Aaron rubbed his forehead. "Can you just get to the point? You don't have to give us the history of portals. I'm not taking your class."

"But I thought..."

"Johnson!" Was that a headache starting behind his eyes? Aaron groaned.

Tristan clicked through a few slides as he sighed and shook his head. "No one appreciates a good lecture these days." He stopped on a collection of accounts. "Drew and I went through the Institute file and called as many witnesses as we could. A few people talked about their experiences while others hung up on us."

"The stories matched our experience. They were at the lake after dark, the ghost appeared, and then the portal. The ones who lost friends saw them disappear inside in a matter of seconds," Drew said.

"That's what I thought." Aaron leaned back in his chair and studied the words on the wall. "I talked to Amanda Perez's sister, Leah, yesterday. She said when she saw the portal, she heard a voice call her name. Did any of these witnesses hear the same?"

"Funny you should ask that." Tristan clicked the remote. A new slide appeared with numbers on it. "Out of the sixteen witnesses who were willing to talk to us, four of them heard someone or something call their names."

"Did any of you?" Aaron asked.

Everyone around the table said no.

He raised an eyebrow. "Even our two psychics?"

"No." McKenna nodded to Tristan. "You?"

"No. But we weren't close to the portal. We were several feet away."

"And these four people all said they stood near it."

"But not near enough to get sucked in?" Aaron rolled his chair closer to the table. His right knee bounced.

"No," Tristan said.

"All the evidence we found, even the disappearances, all

point to March." Drew jumped in. "It only opens on a few nights in March. But it isn't predictable."

"Except when it comes to the years people go into the portal. It's a pattern of every five years," McKenna pointed out.

Aaron dropped his head to the table. "We have all of these bits and pieces of information, but we can't seem to make sense of the puzzle." Hope disappeared by the second. With a sigh, he lifted his head. He turned his attention back to the PowerPoint. "Drew, play the video. Maybe there's something on there that can help us."

Drew nodded, hit play, and sat down in the chair across from Aaron.

The picture shook as the camera captured the expanse of the lake and the dark forest surrounding it. In the dark, everything blurred together. The only source of light came from the one mounted on the camera, and a couple of bobbing flashlights. A young man with floppy red hair and earnest blue eyes stepped into the frame.

He held his arms out. "As you can see, we made it to Laureline Lake with plenty of time to spare. For the record, Jerry came up with the idea." The camera bobbed in acknowledgement.

"Devin, you're taking up the whole shot," a guy off camera yelled.

Devin scoffed and continued with his intro. "According to legend, this lake is haunted and is also a portal to *Hell*." He moved closer to the camera, and his eyes widened on the last word. "We're going to keep this camera running all night to get proof that the legend is real."

Aaron rolled his eyes. He knew guys like Devin. People who investigated the paranormal as if they rode a roller coaster. They hunted for the thrill, the novelty. He thought of the myriad of ghost hunting shows that populated cable.

People like that usually wound up getting themselves hurt. "Can we speed this up?" he asked.

Drew fast forwarded through the rest of Devin's speech. A long stretch of the camera pointing at the lake followed. Then a glowing form sped into the frame.

"Stop." Aaron raised a hand. The fine hairs on his arm stood at attention. Drew pressed play. Amanda walked across the frame as if she were out for a nightly stroll. She seemed to catch sight of the camera and rushed it. The picture went fuzzy. When the picture came back, the camera pointed across the lake, zooming in on a couple of dancing lights. Aaron straightened. He knew those lights, remembered them well. A chill ran over his skin. Around the table, he saw everyone else take notice, too.

"I know those lights," McKenna said.

"The start of the portal," Tristan agreed.

They watched as the lights swirled faster and faster until they became the portal. Everything around the swirling vortex bent toward it as the air sucked in. Devin ran into the shot.

"Devin, get out of there, man!" Someone, maybe Jerry, yelled.

"Don't you hear it?" Devin moved too close. "Somebody's calling my name."

Drew turned the sound as high as it would go. The ghostly sound of a voice calling "Devin," echoed in the quiet room.

Aaron held his breath as he leaned in, studying every detail of the portal as the young man on the screen walked toward it. "Pause it!" Drew did so as Aaron jumped out of his chair. He pointed at a dark shape inside the portal. "What is that?"

McKenna leaned in next to him. "It looks like a person."

Drew hit the play button. In an instant, the dark shape

blinked out of the frame. On screen, Devin lost his footing and flew right into the portal, exactly like Tabitha and her sisters had.

The hole snapped shut in a flash.

Aaron set his jaw. He wanted to study the video frame by frame. He refused to believe the portal ran one way. But the footage captured the proof that Amanda appeared right before it. She charged the camera five minutes before the dancing lights started. The voice and the mysterious shape inside the portal added another element. Aaron speculated that someone fought to get out, or maybe something darker did live in the portal. He raked both hands through his hair as he tried to sort out his thoughts.

Where did he even start with all this information?

"What are you thinking, man?" Drew asked as he stopped the video.

Aaron wanted to walk away and brood in his office instead of facing the four people looking at him. He sat back in his chair as he rubbed his chin. "This case has a lot of moving parts. On the one hand, we have a ghost trapped next to a lake. I feel it's our duty to help her move on."

"I agree," McKenna said.

"On the other hand, we have a portal that goes to another place. Whether it's Hell or a pocket dimension or the other side of the world, I don't know. And my wife is trapped there with her sisters and who knows how many other people."

"Where does the portal go?" McKenna asked.

"The boy on screen hit the nail on the head." Matthew spoke for the first time. Aaron gave the man his full attention. "I don't think it's Hell, but I think it's another world or realm. It's a forest, all gray and foggy."

Aaron's jaw dropped open.

15

A aron popped up his head. "You've seen it? You've been there? How did you..."

Matthew lifted one hand in a placating gesture. "I've never been through the portal, but I've seen it through someone else's eyes. Someone who did go to the other side."

Aaron had so many more questions, but he held back to let Matthew continue. Hope burned in his chest like a bright flame.

"My power works kind of like Tristan's, but I see the present in other locations, and I don't get pulled into it." He sat back and rested his joined hands on his stomach. "I can hold a picture of somebody or one of their belongings and see where they are right at that moment. I didn't advertise it when I worked on the force up in Boone, but most of the people I worked with knew. I'm terrible at hiding things." One corner of his mouth curved up.

"How did you see the other side of the portal?" Aaron asked, hope continuing to spring inside of him.

"About five years ago, a young woman from Boone went

missing, Hannah Page. She camped with her friends at Laureline Lake on a chilly March night and disappeared."

"Her friends must have seen the portal."

Matthew nodded. "Like a lot of other people, the legend attracted them. Hannah got too close." He cleared his throat. "I had one of the hoodies she'd taken on the trip and used it to try to find her. What I saw didn't make any sense. I saw the place through her eyes. Saw the fog, the trees." He gave Aaron a pointed look. "And the monster."

"Monster?" Aaron's stomach sank. "What kind of monster?"

"The big, ugly, black kind with sharp teeth and claws. No other way to describe it. I was so surprised I lost the connection. I told my partner what I saw, but he didn't know of any woods that matched that description. He dismissed the monster, saying I must've seen something wrong." Matthew banged his fist on the table. "But I know what I saw."

"No one's calling you a liar, Dad." Tristan sat down next to him and patted him on the back. "Especially not this group."

Matthew relaxed, opening his fist. He rested his hand, palm flat on the table. "I'm sorry if it sounded like I doubted you, Mr. Johnson. I didn't mean to be disrespectful. It's just, I've never come across a monster before."

Aaron understood. People doubted his accounts as well, even when he had proof to show them. As for monsters, he'd never read about them in any paranormal account before. Fairy tales and stories, yes, but nothing he considered nonfiction. Nor had anyone ever mentioned them in the Institute. In all his investigations, he'd proven the existence of ghosts, but nothing else. However, he kept an open mind about other strange things. "Did you happen to see a way out?"

Matthew shook his head. "Nothing but a cloudy sky and

trees as far as the eye could see. And the portal, stubborn thing, didn't want to open for us." He sighed. "Of course, we visited during the day."

According to Matthew, Tabitha and her sisters had landed in some other realm. Yes, monsters existed there, but it meant she was alive. She wasn't lost in a dark hole or a void or vanished forever. She was somewhere. All he had to do was find a way to get to her.

Aaron picked up the pen next to McKenna's pad of paper and retrieved his own pen. He stood them with their points on the table, holding them upright with his shaking hands. He lifted the left one. "Ghost appears and warns people away." He lifted the other pen. "Then five minutes later, a portal opens, apparently to another world." He surveyed the people around the table. "What is the connection? Is she opening the portal, or does she know when it opens?"

McKenna turned on her phone and flipped through the files. "According to the Institute's notes, the portal legends started in 1975."

"The year after Amanda died," Tristan said. "I felt her death. She drowned. She didn't go through a portal."

"Portals appear near water after a traumatic event," Drew said.

"Like the fabric of the universe can't handle it?" Tristan asked.

Matthew sat forward. "More like the person who died can't handle it."

Aaron set down the pens with a clatter. "Bingo."

"So, what does that mean?" McKenna placed her phone back on the table.

"I think they're connected." Aaron held up a hand. "I know we don't have proof, but I think helping Amanda is our best chance of helping Tabitha."

Drew raised an eyebrow. "Wait a minute. Do you think if

we help Amanda move on, the portal will let go of all the people it's holding?"

"I hope so." Aaron tapped the table with one finger. Fire stoked his temper, pushing the helplessness away. He planned better when he wanted to hit something. "We have information about Amanda, a place to start. But first," he met Matthew's eyes. "Can I ask you to try and look in on my wife? Tell me if she's okay?"

Matthew nodded. "Yes. I want to help in any way I can."

"Then back to Laureline Lake."

***

Monica's bottom lip started to tremble. "I want to go home." She grabbed Tabitha's arm. "Take me home." She sighed. "I should've listened to my friends and not gone near the portal."

Tabitha agreed with Lisa. With the world around them tumbling down, they couldn't stay there. Who knew how long the clearing's safety would hold? Someone had to take charge, and Tabitha thought she should. She took a deep breath, drawing her shoulders back.

"That settles it. We have to find a way out of here. If this place is collapsing in on itself, then I don't think it's a good idea to stick around." She grabbed her coat and her spear. "I say our best bet is to find Amanda and talk to her."

"I told you she doesn't know how to get us out." Eric raked his hands through his hair. He slumped, his expression defeated.

"Either she does or the creepy man I saw in the Victorian does." Tabitha tapped her chin. "The one who knew my name. One of them holds the key to leaving this place."

Devin's eyes widened. "We need to avoid him at all costs."

Questions came to mind, but Tabitha thought better of it. They didn't have the time to waste.

"Amanda, it is. I'm telling you that ghost is hiding something." Tabitha tripped over her words. "She knows she's dead and a ghost. That's rare. But that also means she knows she's stuck, and she's terrified to move on. Plus, she's connected to this portal. It didn't appear until after she died." She looked around at all the faces. The portal and its world revolved around Amanda. "It's time we convinced her to move on."

"We don't know what she's holding onto," Corrie pointed out.

"Then we need to find out." She stamped her foot. "This is what I do. This is what paranormal investigating is supposed to be about. Not the gadgets. Not capturing the evidence of ghosts. Not finding a way to use it to your own advantage. But helping those who were once people find peace. And in the process, get us out of here." She tucked her hair behind her ears as she marched to the tree line. "Grab everything you came with because we're getting out of here."

"And if we don't want to follow you?" Eric asked.

Tabitha glared at him over her shoulder. He stood with his bow and quiver slung around his shoulders. He hooked his thumbs into the pockets of his jeans. He set his mouth in a thin line, his brows down. His negative attitude annoyed her while weighing down the rest of team. "Then stay here and take your chances." She strode into the forest. "I'm going to find Amanda."

Lisa joined her with Corrie and Monica right behind her. "I don't think I've ever seen you like this, baby sis." Lisa patted her on the back. "Let's do this."

Tabitha turned back to Eric, Hannah, and Devin. "I know the world changed. It's probably changed on us, too. I don't know how slow time moves here if it moves at all. But I don't want to leave you behind."

The three of them exchanged another glance. Tabitha didn't know how long they had depended on only each other. After all, they managed to survive when the others disappeared. She waited for their decision, not wanting to push.

Eric nodded. He relaxed his shoulders. "Fine. We'll try it your way."

Tabitha returned his nod. "Thank you." Relief filled her. She hadn't wanted to leave them. It wasn't in her nature.

Tabitha and her sisters waited while the others gathered what meager belongings they had. Devin carried the rest of the spears, Hannah had her bag, and Eric had his bow and arrows. Together, the group left the clearing. Tabitha kept her eyes forward, never turning back.

The foggy forest stretched out with no end in sight. One tree resembled another no matter how far they walked. Tabitha put one foot in front of the other, guessing at the direction. She hoped they found Amanda and soon. She wondered if any other safe clearings existed, especially if they needed to stop and rest. She didn't want to be the reason a monster killed them all.

She studied the others with her. They trusted her to get them home, but how could they when she didn't trust herself?

"Okay, we're here in the woods. How do we find Amanda?" Lisa turned in a complete circle.

"I can." Corrie stepped between them. "I can try to sense her."

"That's a great idea." Tabitha once again felt useless, but she needed all the help she could get.

Corrie inhaled a deep breath and closed her eyes. She stood as still and silent as a statue. Tabitha held her breath, her pulse quickening. The forest froze with her, waiting to see what happened. Not one branch bowed.

Corrie's eyes popped open. "Someone's here."

"We're all here," Eric said, his tone dry.

"No." She turned until her eyes met Tabitha's. "Somebody is with you." She took a step forward. "I sense you and someone else in the same space. It's weird."

Tabitha swallowed, taking a step back. She glanced all around her but saw no one. "Corrie, are you okay?"

She stopped and blinked. "They're gone."

Tabitha looked to her left and right again but didn't see anyone she didn't recognize. "Who was it?"

"I don't know." Corrie shook her head and turned away.

16

D aylight changed the lake from menacing to inviting: bright, welcoming, a fun place to bring the whole family. Sunlight reflected off the water. It was too bad death and a portal to Hell or some other place infested with monsters marred the experience.

The area remained silent. No wildlife hung around the spot. Aaron didn't expect any in the winter, but he figured animals avoided the place all year round.

A woody and damp smell filled the place, adding to the late winter chill.

Aaron stood in the spot where the portal had snatched Tabitha away from him. He reached out, but his hand met nothing but air. A chilly, cool breeze brushed his cheek, a degree warmer than two nights earlier. He scowled at the grass. He hated this place. He turned to face Tristan's father. The older man stood tall, his hands in his pockets. "Whenever you're ready, sir."

Matthew arched a brow. "It's going to take me a minute. I'm a little older and a little slower." He waved Aaron away.

"You're going to have to back up a little, though." He pulled his hands out of his pockets.

Aaron nodded, gave the man Tabitha's camera, and walked closer to the van. He pressed his back against it, crossing his arms. He hoped this would work. Then he'd know if Tabitha was alright or not.

"I feel like I should be doing something," Drew said. He stood beside Aaron, his hands in his coat pockets.

"You and me both."

Matthew clutched the camera and closed his eyes. He walked around in circles, his brow furrowed in concentration.

Aaron chuckled. "Tristan, he really is your dad."

Tristan leaned out of the van. "What do you mean?"

"You both have the same way of using your powers. The weird psychic amble." Aaron shrugged. "At least until you lose it."

Tristan turned his attention back to his father. "Yeah, I guess." He paused for a minute. "Wait. Lose it?"

Aaron waved him off when Matthew raised a hand.

"I see a group of people walking through a forest." His brow furrowed. "Some of them are grumbling, arguing about leaving a clearing." He cocked his head to one side. "They're searching for someone named Amanda."

"The ghost?" Aaron pushed away from the van. "Why look for Amanda inside the portal?"

Matthew ignored the question. "I get the sense the place isn't safe."

Fear crawled up Aaron's spine. "Monsters?" He took a step forward.

"I don't see any."

"Is Tabitha okay?"

"She's okay. I wouldn't be able to see through her eyes if she weren't."

That made him feel a bit better. "What else are you getting? Can you hear anything around her?" He swallowed. "Can you pick up what she's thinking or feeling, like Tristan does with the past?"

Matthew stood still, eyes remaining closed. "No. I don't become the person. A short, blonde woman is trying to sense this Amanda."

"Corrie," McKenna supplied. She sat in the open passenger seat of the van. "She's a medium. Sensing souls is part of her wheelhouse."

"Corrie is coming over to talk to Tabitha." He straightened. "I think she knows I'm here."

"What?"

"She's looking closer. Well, I'll be damned. I think she does know I'm here." His eyes popped open, the connection broken.

"That's it?" Aaron's hope deflated. "Corrie might have noticed you, and you pop out?"

Matthew wiped sweat from his brow. Aaron noticed the older man breathed heavy, and some of his anger dissipated. Matthew found Tabitha. Aaron refused to repay him with a temper tantrum.

"Sorry. Can't hold it as long as I used to. Give me a minute." He let out a big breath. "And there's no 'might have.' She definitely sensed me." He chuckled. "First time that's ever happened to me."

Tristan hopped out of the van and ran over to his father. He led him back, helping him into the backseat. Matthew gave the camera to Aaron.

Matthew tried to push Tristan away. "I'm not that old."

"Yeah, but you still need to sit down. Don't argue with me. If something happens to you, Mom'll have my head."

Matthew laughed again. "She'd skin us both." He wiped

his brow as he settled into the van. He focused on McKenna. "A medium, you said? Makes sense."

McKenna's eyes brightened. "Meaning?"

"She can sense a person's soul. When I do my thing, a part of me is there with the person I'm watching through. So, she might have picked up on my soul."

"Corrie never mentioned being able to do that before." Aaron paced away from the van, made a circle, and returned. He gripped the camera as if it were a lifeline. "Did you see anything else?"

"Your wife and her sisters aren't alone. I saw two men and two other women in the forest with them." Matthew looked Aaron in the eyes. "One of them was Hannah, and she doesn't look a day older than when she disappeared. Saw that red-haired boy from the video, too. I didn't recognize the other two."

McKenna pulled out her phone and showed him a picture of Monica. "Was she one of them?"

"Yeah. She was the other young woman."

"So, wherever they are, they can't age, and it's not safe." Aaron filed away the information. "Anything else? Any monsters like last time?"

Matthew shook his head. "Didn't see any monsters this time, but I got one glimpse." He leaned back into the seat, breathing steadily. "Give me a few more minutes, and I can try again."

"No way." Tristan set his jaw. "That one glimpse took a lot out of you. You're not looking again for the rest of the day."

Matthew raised an eyebrow. "You're in charge now?"

"I'm looking after you."

"I agree with Tristan. I don't want you to overdo it, sir, but I appreciate you looking," Aaron passed the camera to Drew, who placed it somewhere in the van. He turned back to the area where he last saw Tabitha. "Let's figure out what happened to Amanda and see if we can help her move on. Maybe that'll help open the portal."

"Wait a minute." McKenna hopped out of the van. "Mr. Johnson, when you feel ready, do you want to try something crazy?"

Matthew took a gulp from a water bottle Tristan handed him. "Please call me Matthew. We're practically family." He set down the bottle. "And I'm always up for something crazy. What did you have in mind?"

"No. He's wiped out, Mac." Tristan looked from his girlfriend to his father.

"He's already looking better," McKenna protested.

Matthew waved away his son's concern. "Don't mind him. What's your idea?"

Aaron leaned in, intrigued.

"Well, Corrie sensed you, right? And you say a part of your soul is with the person you're watching, right?"

"Go on."

"What if you watched through Corrie's eyes, and she channeled you?"

Matthew's eyes widened. "You're thinking we can get a message to Tabitha through her?"

"Yeah." McKenna's soft face brightened.

Aaron's heart skipped a beat. "Is that possible?" A way to talk to Tabitha lifted his spirits.

"I don't know. That's why it's crazy. Psychic powers behave in weird ways. But if his power works the way he says it does, it's like he's a ghost there. And Corrie channels ghosts." McKenna's hands rested on her hips and pulled her shoulders back in determination. "I think it could work." She nodded to Matthew. "That is, if you're willing to try."

"I am, but we've got another problem. I've never talked to the people I watch. They can't hear me. How do I ask Corrie to help us?" Matthew climbed to his feet, his color coming back.

McKenna pressed her lips together. "You said she sensed you in Tabitha. Maybe she'll sense you in herself?"

"Okay. I'm willing to try." Matthew took a deep breath.

"Dad, please don't overdo it," Tristan wiped a hand down his face as he held onto his father.

Aaron understood Tristan's anxiety. He didn't want to hurt Matthew while trying to help Tabitha. He didn't like pushing a psychic beyond his limits, especially an older one. "Yeah, Tristan's right. We can try later."

"No, we're trying now. I'm fine. I can do this." Matthew stepped away from the van. "Do you have a picture or anything that belongs to Corrie?"

Aaron grimaced. They didn't have anything that belonged to Corrie and most of his pictures lived on his phone. He thought about how long it would take to contact Noah, go to Charlotte, and come back. Laureline Lake was halfway between Charlotte and Asheville. He yanked out his phone.

"It looks like you can rest a little longer, Matthew." He located Noah's number and pressed send.

Noah answer after the first ring. "Aaron! Do you have her? Is she okay?"

Aaron swallowed. "No, but I'm getting close. I need your help."

"Anything."

"I know you're at work, but how fast can you grab something that belongs to Corrie and get to Laureline Lake?"

Noah didn't hesitate. "I'm on my way."

Forty-five minutes later, a sleek silver Jeep rumbled down the gravel road. It parked next to the van. A medium-height man with blond hair, wearing a light blue button-down shirt, black dress pants, and a dark blue tie, stepped out. He carried a stirring spoon. He loosened his tie as he jogged to the group, his blue-green eyes bright.

"Here. This spoon is her favorite to bake with." He practically shoved the spoon into Aaron's hand. "What do you need it for?"

"It's going to sound crazy," Aaron began. He gave the spoon to Matthew, who walked back out to the lake with it.

"My wife channels ghosts. I think I'm used to crazy."

"He's got a point." Drew stuck his head out of the van.

Matthew held the spoon and closed his eyes. He began his psychic amble again.

"Mr. Johnson is going to contact your wife." Aaron watched the older man while holding his breath.

A nything?" Tabitha's legs ached. Her stomach growled, and she would've killed for some water.

The group walked for a long while, following Corrie's vague directions. She'd sense something, and they'd go left. A few minutes later, she'd feel something else, and the entire group changed course. Tabitha knew they probably zig-zagged all over the creepy forest. She didn't know what her sister sensed, but she wasn't a reliable GPS.

Tabitha leaned on the closest tree, resting her shoulder against it. She peered down at the bandage on her scratched arm and wondered if she needed to change it.

"I think she's maybe..." Corrie trailed off, starting in a new direction.

"We need to stop," Eric dropped to the ground. He pulled off his bow and quiver, setting them next to him.

"Oh, thank you. My legs are killing me." Hannah plopped on the dirty ground.

"Do you have any more water or granola bars?" Monica joined her.

Hannah dug through her bag. "I have one bottle of water left, and two granola bars." She pulled them out. "We'll all have to share."

Tabitha sat down next to her. "Are there any other options for food or drink around here? You didn't supply everyone this whole time, did you?" She took the small piece of granola that Hannah gave her.

"No. Back near the clearing, we found a creek that we sometimes drank from, and we took turns hunting for berries through the forest."

"Which we can look for again. I'm just going to need a minute." Eric blew out a breath as he laid down.

Lisa sat down next to him. "This place is like the worst maze ever."

Tabitha lifted her injured arm. "Hannah, can you check this?"

"Sure." She unwrapped the wound with gentle care. She smiled when she pulled the makeshift bandage away. "It's looking good. The bleeding has stopped."

Tabitha peered at the scratches. They no longer hurt and didn't seem an angry red. They still didn't look great, though. Instead of gashes, three long, red welts marred her upper arm. Gingerly, she rolled down the sleeve of her sweater. She sighed when she saw the matching tears in the fabric and the dried blood stains around it. When she got back to the real world, she'd have to throw it out.

Eric stood and strapped his bow and quiver around his body. "Okay, I'm going to hunt for food and water. Everybody, stay here."

"I'll go with you," Lisa offered. "Maybe we can find another part of the creek."

Eric agreed. He held out a hand. Lisa took it and climbed to her feet. Tabitha noticed a look pass between them. They stood closer together and weren't arguing. She wondered when that change had happened. Together, they set off in another direction, promising not to go too far and to keep away from monsters.

Tabitha expected monsters, and they hadn't run into one yet, nor any trouble at all. No aftershocks from the earthquake, either. Things remained quiet and still. A chill slipped down her spine. The forest waited for something, but what?

Tabitha took a sip of the bottled water and passed it to Corrie. "Are you doing okay?"

"Yeah." Corrie sipped. "I'm not too drained, but I keep picking up all sorts of things." She passed the water bottle to Monica. "I don't know if I can zero in on Amanda."

"What kind of things are you sensing?" Devin sat across from them, drawing lines in the dirt.

Corrie drew her brows together. "I don't know. It's like a buzzing. I feel it one moment, and it's gone the next. I can't seem to nail it." She sighed. "It's frustrating." She shivered. "I'm worried it's the other souls. The people who were trapped here and didn't make it."

"You're probably tired. We can rest then you can try again," Monica smiled.

"You're right. I need to take a minute, take a..." she trailed off again, but this time her eyes glazed over.

Tabitha moved to her knees. "Corrie?"

Corrie pressed her lips together, her eyes still unfocused.

"Corrie?"

She closed her eyes. When she opened them, her gaze sharpened. "Tabitha Lawson?" Her sister's voice lowered an octave, but the cadence resonated wrong. Someone different spoke through her. Tabitha remembered the stranger in the Victorian, and her stomach dropped. She feared he'd harm her sister.

Tabitha raised her chin and moved back her shoulders. She fisted her hands at her side. "Who are you? What did you do to my sister?"

Her tone caught the rest of the group's attention.

Corrie held up her hands in surrender. "I'm here on Corrie's permission. I promise." She poked her chest. "I'm Matthew Johnson, Tristan's dad."

Tabitha's fear melted away. "What? How? You're not dead."

"No." Corrie shook her head and chuckled. "No, I'm alive, although my wife worries my cholesterol will kill me. I'm here at the lake with my son, Aaron, Drew, and McKenna. I can see you in the portal. When I tried earlier, your sister sensed me. So, I asked her if I could try talking through her. She said yes." She shrugged. "I've got to say this is weird."

"For you and me both."

"What's happening?" Devin leaned in closer.

"We can talk to the outside world," Tabitha explained.

"I don't know how long I can hold this," Corrie-as-Matthew said. "I can already feel myself fading. Are you all okay?"

"Yeah, we are. Is Aaron okay?"

"He is. He misses you, and now he's yelling at me because I said that."

Tabitha smiled, her heart swelling with joy. "He's okay."

"I want to pass along some information." Matthew proceeded to tell Tabitha everything they knew about Amanda and the portal. Like her, Aaron thought Amanda and the portal were connected to each other somehow. Its energy strengthened every five years, possibly using the people it took. She listened, absorbing the information. The portal kept perfect time for an unthinking phenomenon.

Tabitha told him a shortened version about the monsters,

the stranger in the Victorian, and the earthquake. She down-played the incident in the house. She waited while she assumed Matthew relayed the information. She braced for her husband's reaction.

"Aaron's cussing again."

"I'm not surprised."

Corrie touched her shoulder. "I have to go. This connection is breaking. I'm tired, and so is your sister. But I'll try to contact you again when we know more."

"Thank you."

Corrie closed her eyes and slumped sideways. Tabitha and Monica caught her.

"That was so freaky," Monica said.

"I know."

Corrie's eyes fluttered open. "My head hurts." She put her hand to her temple, wincing.

Hannah passed the water bottle to her. "Here, have the last of it."

Corrie drank it all while leaning against Tabitha. "Thank you."

"No, thank you." Tabitha wrapped her arms around her. "Thank you for letting Tristan's dad talk through you."

Corrie gave her a weak smile. "It was worth a try. I'm glad it worked. I was skeptical when I heard him in my head. I've never channeled the living before."

"I guess there's a first time for everything."

At that moment, all color drained from Corrie's face. Her smile vanished.

Worry jumped into Tabitha's throat. Had the connection been too much for her sister?

"What's wrong?" Monica gripped Corrie's arm.

"Do you sense Amanda?" Hannah asked.

"No, but I'm picking up something dark. Something

wrong." She pointed straight ahead. "It's coming this way and fast."

"Hide," Tabitha pushed to her feet.

Hannah and Devin scrambled to stand. They headed for the nearest trees.

Tabitha and Monica helped Corrie. They headed in the opposite direction, searching for the best cover.

As she crouched behind a thick trunk, Tabitha waited to hear the thundering crunch of the underbrush that signaled the monster. Instead, she heard nothing. But an icy wind blew across her face. She pressed her back against the tree and stared ahead as Monica and Corrie huddled next to her. Corrie wrapped an arm around the terrified teenager.

"It's going to be okay," Corrie whispered.

The cold wind intensified, causing leaves and sticks to rush by. Tabitha pulled her jacket tighter around her. She shivered, and her teeth chattered.

"Tabitha."

Tabitha heard her name on the wind. She glanced at Corrie and Monica, but neither one of them seemed to hear it.

"Tabitha."

It sounded like a song, intoxicating and melodic. Something inside of her urged her to go to the voice. She fought against it, but the pull grew stronger. As the icy wind blew harder, her hair whipped against her face, stinging the skin it touched. The voice rose in pitch and intensity. Tabitha let go of Corrie.

"Tabby, what are you doing?" Her sister sounded so far away.

Tabitha walked around the tree's trunk, leaving Monica and Corrie behind. Out of the corner of her eye, she saw Devin do the same. She didn't acknowledge him, and he didn't acknowledge her. In the back of her mind, she remembered Matthew telling her about Aaron's dark entity theory.

Danger lurked in the forest. She had to turn back, but her body didn't listen.

She walked around trees and through brush until she reached a dark cluster of trees. Their branches twisted and wove together to form a dark opening. She stepped through.

18

Aaron waited beside the lake as Tristan and McKenna saw his dad back to Tristan's apartment. He thanked Matthew so much the older man had to stop him. But passing messages back and forth tired Matthew, and Tristan convinced him to get some rest.

Aaron sat in the dewy grass, watching as the sun set behind the trees. He laid the Institute's report plus his own notes out in front of him. He studied every word, every interview, and every morsel as the light waned. What was he missing? Why had Amanda spent the past forty years haunting the lake? What business held her there? And who was the dark figure in the portal? Did the figure call Devin on the video? Did it match the stranger Tabitha met in her childhood home? Aaron narrowed his eyes. And why did his wife fascinate it?

The idea of a dark entity came back to Aaron. He denied outright calling it a demon. After all, those didn't exist, right? He questioned his own belief. Working at the Institute, he heard stories about possible demons appearing at haunted sites. Things that weren't quite human. The idea chilled him to the bone. But investigators at the Institute loved to exaggerate their experiences, especially if Philip Greene were listening. However, Aaron kept the idea in the mix. He wasn't one to ignore a possibility, no matter how strange it sounded.

Even after the sun set, he pulled out a flashlight and kept reading. He had to figure out what it all meant and if it led to a way out of the portal for Tabitha and her sisters. He raised his head and studied the dark trees. He'd find a way to save his wife, even if it took his whole lifetime.

A light shined in Aaron's eyes. "You've got a line in the middle of your forehead."

Aaron threw up a hand to block it. "Drew, lower that thing."

The light dropped. "Sorry, man." Drew settled next to him in the grass. The sun slipped behind the horizon, leaving little light, and Aaron barely made out his friend's outline. Drew sat with his knees bent and his arms resting on them. His flashlight dangled in his hand. "Any new ideas?"

"No." Aaron turned back to the papers.

They sat in silence with the sound of the trees rustling in the chilly wind. Aaron pulled his coat tighter around him.

"You might be more comfortable in the van. Or we could go back to the office?" Drew suggested.

Aaron tapped his flashlight on the ground. "No. I want to see if Amanda shows tonight." He pulled an old tape recorder out of his coat pocket. "I'm hoping she'll answer some questions through this."

Drew took the tape recorder and inspected it. "I haven't seen one of these in a long time." He ejected the tape with a loud pop. "Cool. Vintage technology."

"I'm surprised you know what that is."

Drew put the tape back in, closing the glass front. "Please. My mom had one of these for a long time. Took us forever to convince her to get a CD player." He gave the tape recorder back. "I'm still trying to teach her how streaming services work."

"Well, I hope this will make Amanda more comfortable."

"Even if it's before her time?"

Aaron sighed. "It's hard to find an eight-track player on such short notice."

Drew pointed his flashlight at the papers. "It's a lot of different parts that don't seem to add up."

"You read it?" Aaron swiveled his flashlight in Drew's direction, careful to keep it out of the other man's eyes.

Drew nodded at the report. "Yeah, I read it. Got a copy from Mac."

Aaron gathered the papers, put them in the file in his lap, and closed it. "What do you think?" Drew acted goofy most of the time, but Aaron valued his insight.

"Well, we have a teenager who runs off in the night to a lake because her boyfriend broke up with her, right?" Drew stretched out his long legs and leaned back on his elbows. "She sat alone at the lake."

"Yeah."

"No one knows what happened that night." Drew leaned his head back, and his hat toppled into the grass. "She's a girl who's been coming to this lake practically her whole life. Why did she slip and fall in? If she can't swim, she knows not to get too close."

"But the police found no evidence of murder." Aaron tapped the file.

Drew pushed himself back into a sitting position and stuffed his hat back onto his head. "True. But what if she still had help getting to the water?" He straightened the bill of his cap. "Tabitha mentioned a strange man, possibly a dark entity in that portal."

Aaron narrowed his eyes at Drew. "What's your point? You're talking in circles."

"Some theories out there connect dark entities to portals."

Aaron raised his eyebrows. "But the portal didn't open until after Amanda's death."

Drew winked and pointed a finger gun at him. "Exactly."

"Are you saying that a dark entity somehow reached out to Amanda and used her death to open the portal?"

"It's a theory."

Aaron turned his whole body toward his friend. "What are you basing this on?"

"As much as it creeps me out, dark entities, or demons if you want to go there, look for weaknesses. Humans have a lot of weaknesses, even when we don't like to admit it. If this world has more than one dimension, and those entities occupy them, they probably like to get into this dimension for that fact alone. Amanda was upset, and with teenagers, that feeling can be a hundred times bigger."

"You're an expert on teenagers?"

"No, but I've spent some time with a preteen, and they can be moody as hell." Drew blew out a breath. "Ella had a meltdown after a boy she liked started talking to another girl."

Aaron smiled at the mention of Drew's girlfriend's ten-year-old daughter. He sighed. He stared at the spot between the trees where the portal had opened. The flat darkness dimmed the world around him. "It's a good theory. If we are facing a dark entity, I don't know how to convince it to give me my wife back. Also, if that portal or dimension is collapsing, we don't have any time at all to figure it out."

"What's your plan?"

Aaron waved the recorder. "Get some information from Amanda and try to convince her to move on. Maybe that'll sever her connection to the portal and make it open."

"Has that ever worked?"

"In my experience, no, but it's worth a try."

"And we're sure this'll make the portal open?"

Aaron's stomach sank. "No." With so little information on portals, he had no idea what to expect. For all he knew, Amanda might cross to the other side, and the portal might stay closed. Tabitha and her sisters and everybody with them would be trapped forever, or at least until the portal fell apart on its own. The thought left a sour taste in his mouth.

Headlights appeared around the bend, pulling him out of his melancholy. Beside him, Drew jumped to his feet. "Maybe Tristan will have better luck tonight seeing what happened, especially since Lisa and Corrie can't see him."

"What's he doing back? I didn't tell him to come back." Aaron stuffed his hands in his pockets, worry eating at him. During the past few months, Tristan gained more control over his abilities, but he couldn't choose what past event he'd see. Or from whose point of view. It depended on the strongest energy in the room, or something like that. Plus, he fought harder to see anything outside as opposed to inside.

"Dude, we're not going to leave you hanging. Not if we can keep trying to help." Drew jogged to the car.

Aaron climbed to his feet, dusting the grass off his jeans. He burrowed into his thick coat. The cold tickled his exposed cheeks. The green F-150 truck parked next to the Restless Spirits van, and the headlights turned off. As Aaron walked closer, he saw the dark outlines of Tristan and McKenna. He trained his flashlight on them. Their flashlights bobbed in return.

"Your dad okay?" Aaron asked.

"Yeah, he said he felt better by the time we got back to the apartment. He's in the chair in my living room with his feet up. He's got his color back."

"Look, I'm sorry. I didn't mean..."

"Not your fault." Tristan stopped Aaron's apologies. "My dad made the choice to try and find Tabitha and connect with Corrie. He knew the risks. This isn't his first rodeo."

"I know, but..."

"Stop. We're good. He's good. He just wished he could do more."

Aaron raked a hand through his hair. He regretted asking a man in his sixties to use his energy and power. He also disapproved of his next action, asking Tristan to peek into the past, but Drew made an excellent point. If Amanda didn't show that night, maybe Tristan could still see something. He opened his mouth.

Tristan beat him to the punch. "Let's see if we can find out more about Amanda."

McKenna squeezed his hand. "Are you sure?"

He nodded. "It's worth a try."

Aaron stuffed the folder under one arm and hooked a thumb in his jeans. "I can't ask you to do this."

Tristan's green eyes glared at him. "No one's asking me anything. Although, I don't know if I'll get anything. I don't pick up much when I'm outside."

"What about when you saw Lily's death?" Aaron asked.

"I had her hair clip in my hand. I think I pulled energy from that." Tristan held out his empty hands. "I don't have anything of Amanda's."

Aaron glanced around the quiet dark lake and surrounding woods. "Maybe Amanda will grace us tonight, and I can talk to her. You won't have to do anything."

"Or she could give me a boost," Tristan said. With both the White Lady and the ghost of Drew's ancestor, they learned that ghosts had a way of either taking or boosting a psychic's power. McKenna had been studying the phenomenon during the slow winter, but she hadn't come to any conclusions as to how it all worked.

"Okay, let's do this." Tristan raked a hand through his curls. He then stuffed a hand into his coat pocket, trained his flashlight on the ground, and made his way around the right side of the lake to the place where they were when he had the last vision.

Aaron stood off to the side with Drew as they watched their friend walk in circles, trying to get a feel for the place as quiet blanketed the early spring night. Frogs and crickets hadn't yet come out to find their mates, but Aaron imagined mating didn't happen too often around the lake in the spring and summer. According to reports, the lake gave off a strange vibe all year round.

Throughout his ghost hunting career, Aaron had seen how a few different psychics work. Some of them stared off into space with unfocused eyes. Others looked him dead in the eyes while making their predictions. Tristan walked around like he drank one beer too many, holding his hands out to steady himself, much like his father had earlier that day. When he did get a vision, his whole demeanor changed, depending on the person he connected to. If the person's energy was strong, that person took him over completely. He not only saw the past, but he also channeled it.

For a solid hour, Tristan circled, circled, and circled. McKenna stood off to the side, her gaze on him. Even though it looked like Tristan had all of her attention, Aaron knew she monitored everyone else's emotions, too.

Tristan stopped and sighed. "I'm not getting anything." He lifted his head. "The space is too open, and Amanda isn't around."

Aaron rubbed the back of his neck. The frustration and the waiting killed him. "Nothing? Not an impression or anything?"

"I'm sorry." Tristan shook his head. "I need something of Amanda's to focus. Or the ghost herself here."

"Or the portal," McKenna added. "You saw pieces of her murder when the portal opened."

Tristan nodded. "The power boost."

Aaron wrapped his coat tighter around himself—the later it got, the colder it got. "So, what you're telling me is we have no way to finish Amanda's business, send the ghost into the light, and save my wife?"

"And do it all before the portal stops showing up this year," Drew chimed in.

"Thank you for that reminder." Aaron's voice dripped with sarcasm. No one knew better than he did that he had less than a month. He ground his teeth.

As he turned to head back to the van, a white glow appeared out of the corner of his eye. Aaron whipped his head to the left. Amanda watched him like she planned to paint him. She floated next to him, her gaze inscrutable. Tossing his flashlight to the ground, he stalked toward her.

"Aaron, what are you doing?" McKenna yelled.

"You see her?"

"Yeah."

"Tristan, do your thing. I'm going to talk to her."

"Aaron!" McKenna said something else, but Aaron ignored it.

Amanda didn't move or disappear. She stayed in one spot, hovering by the edge of the trees. She cocked her head to the side and gave him an unblinking gaze.

Aaron yanked out the tape recorder, pressing play. "Open the damn portal!" Aaron demanded. "Give me my wife back!" She didn't answer. She didn't give any indication that she heard him, but he concluded she caught his words. He'd seen ghosts react to sounds around them; some just couldn't seem to talk back without assistance. "Where are Tabitha and her sisters?"

Amanda continued to stare at him with no attempt to communicate.

"Can you hear me? Understand me?"

Nothing.

Aaron gritted his teeth. His whole body cried out for a cigarette at that moment. "Answer me, dammit!"

A blast of wind knocked him sideways. He dropped the tape recorder as he fought for balance.

"Aaron!" He couldn't tell who yelled at him as the wind roared in his ears.

The portal opened right on top of him. He had been so focused on Amanda that he hadn't realized where he halted. He glanced over his shoulder to see Drew running to him. Tristan seemed locked in a vision, and McKenna had a hold of him. Tristan probably had something that might help, and in turn, could help Tabitha. He turned back to the portal. Tabitha remained on the other side, so close.

Pressing his lips together, Aaron ran and jumped inside before he changed his mind.

19

A t first, nothing but darkness surrounded her. Then light and shapes appeared. Tabitha blinked once, twice, and the world came into sharp focus. She sat up in slow increments. Her head and back ached. She wiped her eyes as she looked around. She froze in surprise.

Home. She rested at home in her bedroom with light green walls and dark hardwood. The sheets and blankets on her own king-sized bed cocooned her legs. Soft and warm, she didn't want to move. After a few minutes, Tabitha threw off the covers and placed her bare feet on the cold hardwood floor. It creaked under her weight. She bounced a couple of times to make sure she had heard the squeak.

Disoriented, she crossed to the window to see bright sunshine and green trees. She lifted the window, breathing in the fresh, clean mountain air. With the pleasant temperature, she guessed early summer arrived, maybe late spring. But the season seemed wrong.

She tried to remember what happened before this. She and her sisters fell through a portal, separated from Aaron. She tried to find her way back. Running her fingers through her hair, she tried to piece it all together. Had it been a dream after all? Or had they made it back? She placed her palm flat on the warm glass. Did Aaron find a way to save her? If so, why couldn't she remember how she got home? A coldness settled in her chest. Something inside of her told her the scene didn't make sense.

"There you are." Aaron bounced into the room, a bright smile on his handsome face. His brown eyes sparkled. "I waited for you to get up." His grin widened. "You slept for a long time."

"You did?" Tabitha thought the statement and his tone sounded strange, but she chose to ignore it.

"Sure. We're going for a drive on the parkway, remember? You're going to take pictures. I'm going to get in some fishing." He came up behind her, wrapping his comforting arms around her. He planted tiny kisses on the side of her neck, tickling her and making her giggle.

Tabitha leaned back against him, basking in his warmth. After a nasty dream about being separated from him, she nestled in his arms. She needed this. She needed him. It felt like she'd wandered in the desert without water for so long. But she didn't wander anymore. Aaron made everything better.

"Since when did you take up fishing?" She turned and stood on her toes. She kissed his lips, ready for the zing she always experienced to zip from her head to her toes. No zing. A hollowness followed. Tabitha jerked back, pulled out of her fuzzy happiness. She tried again, pressing her lips to his. He kissed without any feeling behind it. Everything appeared out of focus. She lined up the perfect shot, but the lens refused to sharpen.

"What's wrong, baby? I've always liked fishing." Aaron grabbed her hand. With a flourish, he twirled her. Before she knew it, he pulled her into a waltz. They spun around the room.

Tabitha yanked free and took a full step back, breaking his hold. "No. No, you haven't. Hiking and reading, yes. But not fishing." Aaron didn't like to fish because he said it was boring. He didn't enjoy sitting in the same spot for hours staring at a pole. She remembered the first time he said that, when a friend had asked him to go one summer. Why would he all of a sudden want to do it?

Aaron grasped her hands. Smooth fingers curved around hers with no warmth. His grip tightened. "Well, I do now. This is our new normal. Weekends just for us." He smiled, but it didn't reach his eyes.

The coldness Tabitha felt earlier spread through her arms and legs. Goosebumps appeared on her skin. "What about Restless Spirits?" Most of their investigations happened on Friday and Saturday nights. Since a majority of their clients wanted their homes investigated, the weekend turned out to be the best time. After all, people who worked during the week could leave for a weekend much easier than on a weeknight. Aaron always had something planned.

"What about it? We don't ghost hunt anymore. It's the normal life you always wanted." He dipped his head, and his brown eyes flashed. His smile turned sinister. "I gave it all up for you."

Tabitha gasped as he squeezed her hands. "Stop. You're hurting me." Her hands started to ache. She fought against his hold, tugging until she pulled her hands out of his. She ran around to the other side of the bed, putting as much distance between them as she could. "This isn't real." Aaron loved his job, and she'd never ask him to give it up for her. He'd never quit everything to go fishing.

"Of course, it is." The sinister smile disappeared as quickly as it came. His smile bounced back to bright and cheerful, weird all on its own. "I don't know what you're worried about." He took a step toward her. "We've got so much time to catch up on." He offered his hand. "Work and the business consumed all my time. I forgot what mattered. You matter. Stay with me."

Tabitha backed up into the wall. Yes, she mattered to him, but so did his investigations and his clients. And the ghosts. Especially the ghosts. "You're not Aaron."

Aaron paused. "Yes, I am. Are you feeling okay?" Concern crossed his face as he started to move again.

Tabitha dodged him and ran for the bathroom. She slammed the door behind her, locking it. "You're not Aaron, and this isn't real."

The voice calling her name. The trees that formed a doorway. It all came back to her in bits and pieces.

The doorknob jiggled. "Tabitha, open the door."

"That right there. You rarely ever call me Tabitha." She pressed her back to the door, cold seeping under her skin. "You're not Aaron. I don't know who you are, but you're not him." Her hands trembled as she pushed them against the door.

"Tabitha, you're not playing right," Aaron said through gritted teeth. The whole door shook so hard she thought the hinges might break.

She couldn't hold the door forever. Tabitha jumped away. She scrambled for the small window across the tiny room. She unlocked the locks at the top and tried to slide it open. It refused to move. She pushed with everything she had, but still nothing. She whirled, searching for anything that might break the glass apart.

At that moment, the door burst open, shattering into tiny pieces that flew across the small room. Aaron stalked inside, murder in his dark brown eyes. "You're ruining the game."

"What game?" He'd trapped her with no way out and

nowhere to go. She needed to think, to figure all of this out. How did she get there? What the hell was going on? The voice. The doorway.

The anger in Aaron's eyes seemed to melt away. He visibly relaxed and the carefree smile returned. It scared her more than the anger had.

"Tabitha." He reached for her. She flinched as cold fingers caressed her arm. "This world is yours. You can have whatever you want, whenever you want. You can stay here forever."

She flattened her back against the frigid, tiled bathroom wall. "This world?" None of it made any sense. The voice. The doorway.

"Yes. It's been your world since you stepped through the portal." The cold fingers wrapped around her arm and tightened their grip. Tabitha winced as the cold burned.

"Just fall into the fantasy, like the others. Nothing can hurt you here, not if you want it to." The walls around her fell away. Her bathroom, her bedroom, and her house disappeared into the darkness. "Stop fighting, and you'll have everything you ever wanted."

Tabitha tried to pull away. "No. This isn't right." The woods. She remembered the woods, the fog. She ran with her sisters and the others, looking for Amanda. She wanted to find a way home. A voice called her. It surrounded her as she walked toward an opening made of bent and twisted trees. It whisked through her. She fought to ignore it. She remembered everything.

"I'm not giving up," Tabitha whispered.

Aaron changed, grew taller, thinner. The stranger from her childhood home stood before her. His black hair framed a pale, handsome face. He raised dark eyebrows. "No. It's not giving up. It's letting the place take you." He pulled her closer. "Joining me. I know what you're going through, how you feel. The spare sister. Never good enough for your daddy. The supportive wife to your husband. He's so focused on his business that he's never really appreciated what your dreams are. He's never appreciated you."

"That's not true." The words barely made it past her lips as the doubt crept in. Aaron did always put the business first. When was the last time they had taken a trip, just the two of them?

Memories of her father brushing her aside in favor of her older sisters, one with a talent for tech and one who could channel ghosts. The darkness around her shifted. In the next moment, she found herself in her father's study. The stranger let her go and stepped away. She turned to see her father glare at her from behind his desk.

"Tabitha." He steepled his fingers. "I'm worried about you. You don't seem to bring anything to the family business."

"But the pictures, Daddy. I caught the ghost." She rushed forward and pointed out the amazing shot of a female ghost hovering in a doorway.

Philip sighed. "Yes, a lucky shot. One of the few clearer pictures I've seen of a ghost, but anyone can get lucky with a camera. I've gotten shots like this before." He sat back. "You need to get better, or I don't know what we'll do with you."

Tabitha's heart sank. She remembered this moment. She had been fourteen and had finished her first hunt with her sisters. She thought the investigation had gone well. A full apparition, right there in front of her, framed in that doorway. The ghost fascinated her instead of scaring her. She had raised the camera to her eye and snatched the shot, but none of it mattered. Her father had tossed the picture aside like it meant nothing.

A cold hand touched her back. She shivered.

"See," the stranger said. "Here, it doesn't matter what he thinks. You can make this world your own. Give in."

Tears burned her eyes as she fought to hold them back. She thought she had put those doubts away, showed the world their feeling about her never affected her. But the thoughts lived in the back of her mind, crushing her the same in that moment as they hurt the fourteen-year-old version of her. Worthless. She was worthless.

She curled her hands into fists. She refused to believe those thoughts again. "No. This world isn't real." She whirled to face him, her heart pounding in her chest. "Who are you?"

He cocked his head to the side, his black eyes contemplative. "I don't have a name. Or if I did, I don't remember it."

"What do you want from me?"

He flashed sharp teeth. "Your darkness. Your light. Everything you are." He hissed. "Humans are fascinating, maddening." He licked his lips. "Delicious."

"Are you a demon?" Tabitha swallowed. Growing up, she'd heard stories—the dark ones no paranormal investigator wanted to admit. Stories about hauntings that chilled the investigator to the bone.

"What an interesting word." He laughed. It raked against her ears like nails on a chalk board. "I like it. Maybe I'll use it." He grabbed her upper arms and whipped her around to face the dark again. "Let's see what else the real world has for you."

20

Her father and his study vanished into the darkness. The world shifted around her until she perched at the two-person kitchen table in the small apartment she shared with Aaron in Charlotte. The white walls, off-white carpet, and tiny space brought back so many memories. A younger version of Aaron sat across from her, his brown eyes eager. He wore his hair a little longer back then.

"What do you think? Our own paranormal investigation business?" He pushed the business plan across the table to her. She picked it up and studied it. Although it didn't weigh anything, it felt heavy in her hands.

"A defining moment." The demon flew to her side in an instant, black eyes flashing. He leaned over her, much too close for comfort. "You could've told him you didn't want to do it anymore. You could've told him you wanted to concentrate on photography." He sneered at the younger Aaron.

"But that's not entirely true. I wanted him to follow his dreams." Tabitha studied her husband across the table. He sat there, frozen in the moment, his smile brightening his face.

His brown eyes wide and excited. She knew the hunt wasn't the only reason Aaron loved the job. He loved helping the lost souls they found. It was his way of doing good in the world.

"But he didn't ask you about yours, did he?"

She set down the plan. "The idea made sense. We investigate our own way, focusing on more on people than the paranormal."

"Oh, how boring." Icy breath brushed her ear. "You don't want to do that forever. Taking pictures of ghosts? Trying to prove things that can't be explained?"

She bristled. "Helping people cross over to the other side, whatever that side may be."

The demon draped his arms on either side of her, pressing his white hands on the table. "Think of all of the beauty you capture with your camera. Photos splashed across magazines around the world. Maybe even adorning walls in galleries."

Tabitha shivered as she thought about it. The demon hit a nerve. Aaron didn't ask her if she wanted to do it, but he did ask what she thought about it. Had she told him the truth? Or had she told him what he wanted to hear? She fought to keep resisting the demon's promises, but it weighed on her. She considered giving in and letting go.

"You can make that happen?" She trembled at the thought of a gallery filled with her photographs.

"Anything can happen here. Give in. Stay with me. All of your dreams will come true." The demon moved away, taking the cold with him.

The world around her shifted again, and she found herself at the lake on that long ago night with her sisters. The night she screwed up the first investigation of Amanda and the portal. The chilly night bit into her wet skin and hair as she tightened her coat around her. She braced herself, anticipating her sisters' reactions.

"It's gone, Tabby! Just gone!" Lisa shoved a recorder back into its bag. "All of our hard work for nothing." She zipped the bag and put it into the van. "I have no data, nothing." She whirled on Tabitha. "You don't do anything but get in the way."

"I said I was sorry." Tabitha wrapped her arms around herself and turned to Corrie.

"I'm sorry, Tabby. The portal closed." Corrie shrugged. "We missed it."

"What about next year? It happens every March, right?" Tabitha grasped at straws. A knot of dread tightened in her stomach. She hated letting her sisters down.

"There's no guarantee. Some years it appears frequently; other years, none at all. I'll have to calculate it all over again." Lisa scowled. She broke down one of her data machines. Tabitha didn't know what it did, exactly.

"But, Lisa..." Every word stung as much as it had that night. Lisa's anger. Corrie's disappointment. She started questioning her role in the paranormal investigations that night. But she stuck with it because of her family and Aaron. Was that enough now? Or did she still get in the way?

The demon stepped in front of her and held out a hand. "Do you know I saw you for the first time that night? I knew you needed me, like I need you. I wanted to call to you then. I tried." He peered down at her with his piercing black eyes. "I can make it all better. Come with me."

She raised her hand without thinking. It sounded so easy. No one else needed her. She got in the way. She brought no skills to the investigations. Staying in this world forever made sense. She studied the man in front of her. He seemed sincere, his words holding many different promises. If she gave in, she'd have everything she ever wanted. Her fingers brushed the tips of his.

"Tabby!" A familiar voice broke through. She jumped at the sound of it. "Tabby!" It got stronger with every minute. She pulled her hand away.

"Aaron?" She stepped away from the demon, the trance broken. She paced in a circle but didn't see him anywhere. "Aaron!" She sucked in a breath as hope returned. Her skin warmed.

The lake disappeared, leaving only the darkness. Aaron's voice kept pushing through. "Tabby!" He sounded so close.

She heard him! Another trick? The demon appeared confused and unsure, no longer smiling or smug. The real Aaron called her name, searching for her. Somehow, his voice penetrated the dream world. The demon promised lies. Aaron did need her. She meant something to him. He loved her. Her team and her family needed her. She brought all sorts of experience and skills to the investigations. If she stayed in the portal, she'd die.

Tabitha wished she had something to fight with. She backed further away from the demon and searched the darkness. How did one stop a demon?

"You won't find anything. I'm in control." The demon bared his sharp teeth again, reminding her no humanity existed in him. He had never been human. The rumors about dark entities were true, and she didn't want to mess with this one any longer.

"But all of these memories are mine, which means you're in my head." Something clicked, and Tabitha decided to try something. She imagined a softball bat in her hand. She pictured the round handle, the weight and heft of it. Something cool and solid pressed against her palm. She curled her fingers around it. When she looked down, she held a plain, metal bat.

She played the worst of anyone on her softball team, but she knocked a few balls out of the park during her one and only season in elementary school. Lifting the bat, she pulled back.

"Wait!" The demon held out his hands, and then he transformed into Aaron. "You won't hit your husband."

"You're not my husband." She swung with everything she had. She hit the demon in the head. He staggered backwards, shaking. He shed Aaron's form and became a dark mist. He shuddered before flying at her. Tabitha ducked. The mist dived. She swung. The bat sailed through the mist, scattering it.

The mist shrieked. Tabitha winced as the sound pierced her ears. The mist became a man and grabbed her wrist. He squeezed. Tabitha gasped at the sharp pain, but she held on to her bat.

"You don't have to make this difficult," he hissed.

"Let me go. You don't own me." She punched him in the stomach.

He broke into mist once again.

The world shattered around her.

21

Tabby?" Aaron winced at the crack in his voice from calling her name. He swore he had yelled it for hours, but he hadn't gone far. The woods stretched out in every which way. Bare trees covered the vast area, and everything looked the same. Each time he chose a direction, he hoped it led to Tabitha. He hadn't found any sign of her yet.

He tried to remember all the things he'd read about ghost portals, but none of the books, articles, or websites mentioned a foggy forest landscape. He studied what he saw of it, keeping Matthew's warning about monsters in the back of his mind. He stayed alert as he stomped through his surroundings.

His father loved to camp, and whenever he had the time, they camped all over the Blue Ridge and the Great Smoky Mountains. The landscape surrounding him reminded him of one of those camp sites. A quiet area, a place a person could hang a hammock in the trees. Even though no camp site appeared, it still resembled those places.

Aaron stood in the middle of the forest with his hands

balled into fists at his side. Every direction resembled another. No rules governed this world, making it different from the real one. He jumped through the portal in the dark, and gray light bathed the forest when he arrived. In the time he'd been there, the light never changed.

Movement out of the corner of his eye caught his attention. He turned, and his mouth dropped open. The man walking through the trees had a face he hadn't seen in two years. Tall and lean with light brown skin, blue-gray eyes, and short, dark hair. His expression hardened to stone.

Aaron took an involuntary step back. "Kevin?"

"It's your fault, man. Your fault." Kevin raged as he dodged around the trees.

"What? How are you here?" He remembered the last day he saw Kevin Searcy alive all too well. It happened on the investigation he didn't like to talk about. The one involving a ghost with a taste for killing, and one he never told his current team about. It had been his fault. If he hadn't made a crucial mistake, Kevin would still be alive; he'd failed to protect his best friend. The memory of the light leaving his eyes haunted Aaron.

Aaron's stomach twisted into knots.

Kevin reached him in the blink of an eye. He clamped his hands on Aaron's throat, squeezed, and lifted him off the ground.

Aaron grabbed his friend's forearms and tried to pry him off as Kevin cut off his air. He swung his legs, aiming for his adversary, but Kevin only pressed harder. Aaron buckled under his strength. The edges of Aaron's vision darkened. He prepared to pass out, probably die, and he'd never see Tabitha again. His team would never know what happened to him. A mistake from years before that haunted him fought to kill him.

Screw that! Aaron refused to give up. He kicked out, his

foot connecting with Kevin's stomach. Kevin's hold released, and Aaron dropped to the ground. Kevin doubled over, groaning and holding his middle.

When he hit the ground, Aaron rolled to his feet. The person who attacked him wasn't Kevin, of that he was sure. He remembered Kevin Searcy as a quiet, unassuming friend. They met when Aaron joined the Greene Institute and found themselves assigned to the same team. Kevin was the first psychic Aaron had ever worked with, and he had been good. Aaron blamed himself for Kevin's death, and he never liked to talk about it.

This person was not Kevin.

Aaron rubbed his aching neck as he searched the area for any kind of weapon. A big, thick stick lay on the ground a few inches away. Better than nothing. He crawled to it and closed his fingers around the rough bark. A sneakered foot stepped down on the other end.

"You owe me!" Kevin roared, his eyes glowing red.

Aaron knew he owed Kevin, but he fully realized this wasn't Kevin.

The eyes gave away the truth. The Kevin he remembered brawled beside him, not against him. The real one never choked him to death, bent on revenge. Aaron wheeled and swept the thing's leg out from under it. It hit the ground hard, landing on its back with a thud. Leaves and dust swirled around it. Aaron snatched the stick, stood above Kevin, and held it over his head. His arms and legs tensed as nerves danced in his stomach. He narrowed his eyes, preparing for the next strike.

"We'll hunt you," the thing that looked like Kevin promised as it gnashed pointed teeth.

"Try it." Aaron swung the stick down.

Kevin evaporated into nothing before the stick struck the ground. Aaron stumbled back and took in the vast forest.

Adrenaline pumped through him, his heart racing. He held the stick aloft, twisting and glancing at every sound. What other surprises did this place have in store?

"What the hell?" Aaron lowered his stick as he tried to calm down. He pressed a hand against the rough bark of the nearest tree. He took one breath, then another, as air returned to his lungs. Bit by bit, he relaxed but continued to stay alert.

Then the earthquake started.

Matthew had said the world was unstable, but he hadn't prepared for something like this. He dropped the stick and wrapped his arms around the tree. He held on as tight as he could, his heart in his throat. He hoped nothing fell on him. Trees crashed to the ground around him, the deafening sound crowding in his ears.

When he thought he couldn't hold on anymore, the earthquake stopped.

The instant quiet wracked his nerves.

Gingerly, he peeled away from the tree. He saw devastation all around him, but nothing touched the circle where he stood.

"Consider yourself lucky!" A voice called from behind him.

Aaron turned to see a young man with bouncy red hair treading through the fallen debris. The man looked up to reveal hazel eyes. Aaron narrowed his own eyes. He recognized the redhead. He was the young man from the video. Still, he remained on his guard.

"How so?" he asked.

Branches snapped under the young man's feet. "This place is crumbling in on itself." He shook his head. "It had a good run, but I guess it must be time." When he reached Aaron, he pushed the floppy hair out of his eyes. "I'm Devin."

"Aaron." He nodded to the other man.

Devin stood maybe an inch shorter with a stocky build. He wore a black T-shirt and a pair of jeans. His pale face held a perpetual grin. His name rang a bell, and Aaron realized he was right about him being the man on the videotape, the one who'd disappeared in 2015. Still, Aaron doubted that Devin was who he said he was. After the fake-Kevin's attack, he didn't trust anything in the forest.

"How long have you been here?" Aaron made sure he had his back to the tree while he kept Devin in his sightline.

Devin shrugged. "A few months, maybe. I can't tell. The time of day never changes."

"Are you alive?"

Devin lifted his eyebrows. "As far as I know. You?"

"As far as I know."

Devin took a step back. "Wait. You might be one of those things lurking around here, waiting to kill me."

"Those things?"

"Monsters, people from your past."

"You might be one of those things," Aaron countered.

"I'm not one of those things. That I can promise." Devin hunched as he surveyed the forest. "This place is full of stuff out to kill you."

"Why?"

"Who knows?" Devin shrugged. "Look, if you're not one of those things, and you're really from the outside world, then we need to move. A monster will eventually show up." He sliced his hand through the air. "Trust me. You don't want to be here when they arrive." He swallowed. "You can't kill them, and it's damn hard to make them go away."

Aaron thought of the monster that looked like Kevin and shuddered. He distrusted Devin, but he'd run out of options. Besides, the Kevin Thing attacked immediately. Devin hadn't done anything but talk. Squaring his shoulders, Aaron moved away from the tree.

"Which way?" he asked.

Devin pointed to the way behind him. "I hear there's a clearing back this way. We'll be safe there." He started in that direction.

Aaron fell in step beside him. "I'm looking for my wife. The portal pulled her in about a week ago. She's short with blonde and purple-streaked hair and blue eyes. Her name's Tabitha."

Devin looked thoughtful for a moment, his brow creasing. He moved a low-hanging branch out of the way. "I think I saw her. Was she with two other blondes?"

"Yeah. Those are her sisters. They came through, too."

The redhead shook his head. "I'm sorry, man. The last time I saw her, monsters got to her."

Aaron slammed his hand into Devin's chest, stopping his progress. "Where?" His tone was deadly.

"You don't want to go there, man. She's probably already dead."

Aaron's fingers gripped Devin's shirt. "Where?" he growled, deep and low.

"Back that way." Devin jerked a thumb behind him. "But it's not safe."

"I don't care. Take me there." Heat rushed over him. The muscles in his arm bunched. It took everything not to punch the punk right then and there. A monster was attacking Tabitha right at that moment, and this kid was chatting like nothing happened.

"Are you crazy?" Devin tried to pull away. "I told you. It's not safe."

"Take me, or I'll pound you into the ground." Aaron forced his words through clenched teeth.

Devin pressed his lips together. "Fine. I'll take you as far as I can, but then you're on your own."

"Fine with me." Aaron let him go. He remembered he left

his stick behind and swore. He had no weapon. Groaning, he kept an eye out for another stick. "Lead the way."

Devin huffed out a breath and started walking back the way he came. Nothing but the swish of their legs pushing through the underbrush echoed in the otherwise quiet forest.

After a while, Aaron couldn't take the silence. "What kind of monsters lurk here? Do they all look like people from your past?"

"No. Some are big. Some are man-sized. All of them are nasty."

Aaron's jaw twitched. "And you left my wife alone with one?" He curled his right hand into a fist.

"I didn't know what else to do."

Aaron didn't want to think about how the monster planned to kill his wife. He imagined painful and slow were part of it. He shook his head. If he let his thoughts go down that road, he'd never be able to save Tabitha.

They continued the trek in silence until it felt like they'd been walking a while. Aaron sighed as his leg muscles started to ache. His dry throat begged for water. He glanced around, noticing how the trees all appeared the same.

"This is it!" Devin announced.

Aaron stopped and looked around. Nothing but bare trees surrounded them. No one was in the area.

"Where is she?"

"I don't know." Devin seemed baffled. "I swear they were here."

"Did the monster take them somewhere else?"

"No." Devin's eyes seemed to darken. His posture went from laid back to alert in a split second. He cocked his head to the side. "Tabitha isn't with the monster. She's with the one who rules this place."

"What are you talking about?" Aaron stepped back, his shoulders tense.

"He wants her, and you're not supposed to be here." A creepy smile spread across Devin's face. "But he'll take care of you, too."

Before Aaron could move, Devin smashed his fist into Aaron's face. He fell to the ground, and the world disappeared.

Tabitha jerked awake. The fog and the trees greeted her, a blessed sight. She welcomed the hard, dirty ground she lay on. Something like glittering glass spread all around her on the ground. The fake house and the fake sunlight were gone. Pushing to her feet, she wondered how she'd gotten there. Corrie, Monica, and Hannah were missing. She found herself alone.

She shuddered as she remembered the demon. Something intelligent and terrifying lived in the forest—something that decided he liked her and thought she had a quality he wanted. Something she didn't want to cross again.

She wanted to lay back down to nap right then and there. Her adrenaline rush had left her exhausted. But anything could be lurking around the next turn. A monster. The demon. Somebody from her past trying to kill her. Using the trees for balance, she walked out of the underbrush.

A scuffle ahead of her caught her attention.

Lisa pushed Hannah against a tree, her stick at the younger woman's throat. "Where is she? Where is my sister?"

Corrie, Eric, and Monica burst out of the brush. Corrie

grabbed Lisa's arm. "Lisa, calm down." She struggled to push the stick away from Hannah's throat.

"I don't know." Hannah pushed so hard against the tree that Tabitha thought she'd try to disappear into it. "We tried to stop her, but she walked off."

"She's telling the truth," Corrie continued to fight Lisa.

"Lisa!" Tabitha jogged toward her, hoping she could diffuse the situation. She didn't want to see anyone get hurt because of her.

Lisa's head whipped in her direction. She let Hannah go, dropped the stick, and charged across the forest. She pulled Tabitha into a rib-crushing hug.

The force knocked the air out of Tabitha's lungs.

"Holy shit! I thought I lost you again." She pushed Tabitha away but kept her hands on Tabitha's forearms. "Stop walking off by yourself." She shook Tabitha with every word, her eyes wide.

Tabitha's teeth rattled in her head. "I'm not a child. I can take care of myself."

"That doesn't mean I don't worry." Lisa released her. She glanced at Hannah. "I'm sorry for doubting you." She sighed. "This whole place is making me crazy."

Tabitha straightened her clothes. "It's making all of us crazy." She looked over her shoulder to see the trees unbend as the strange, dark entrance disappeared. She swallowed as a chill ran down her spine.

Corrie moved in for a hug. "You scared me. When I saw you walk off, I tried to stop you. I ran after you and called your name, but you didn't hear me." She stepped back. The worry still hovered in her eyes.

"I talked to him," Tabitha jerked her thumb to the opening that no longer remained.

"Who?" Monica creased her brow.

"The stranger. The one from the house." She told them

about her encounter with the dark entity in a house the resembled the one she currently lived in and how he tried to talk her into giving up. She left out how he seemed attracted to what he called her darkness. She didn't know how to explain it.

She shivered as she remembered his cold touch and how he tempted her for a moment.

Lisa crossed her arms, shuffling from foot to foot. "I thought dark entities weren't real."

"So, did I. It looks like this dimension has one." Tabitha worked to make sure her voice sounded calmer than she felt.

Corrie rubbed her arms. "I knew I felt something wrong." She shivered. "Can you imagine what Dad would do if he found out dark entities were real?"

Lisa swallowed. "I don't want to think about it."

Tabitha agreed. She closed her eyes, trying not to reflect on some of the things her father had done.

"What's a dark entity?" Hannah asked.

Tabitha opened her eyes, focusing on the other woman. "The theory is it's something from another dimension, or Hell itself, that wants to get into ours. Some people think they're demons or the Devil. No one knows for sure."

Monica shuddered. "I don't want to mess with any of that."

"Then you're right. We do need to get out of here." Eric pressed his mouth into a thin line. He had been so quiet the entire time Tabitha forgot he was there.

Lisa turned on him. "Why didn't you tell us about this?" She spat out the question with her usual fire.

"I didn't know." Eric took a step toward her.

Lisa pointed her stick at his chest. "What else are you hiding? Are you working for him?"

Eric knocked the stick out of the way. He puffed out his

chest and glared down his nose at her. "I'm not hiding anything. And who am I supposed to be working for?"

"The entity." The stick found its way back to his chest.

This time he didn't bother moving it. "I'm not working for a dark entity." He touched Lisa's hand. "I promise."

Lisa narrowed her eyes. "Yeah, you conveniently didn't tell us about the dark entity that almost killed my sister." She tapped his chest with the stick. "And you've been here the longest."

"I'm telling you, I've never seen him!" Eric pushed past her, knocking the stick out of the way. Corrie, Hannah, and Monica stepped in front of him.

"Bullshit," Corrie said.

Tabitha raised her eyebrows. Her middle sister rarely used curse words.

Eric sighed and turned a full circle. All five women surrounded him. "Look. I've fought monsters and people from my past. I've never met a dark entity." When no one commented, Eric shoved his thumbs into his pockets. "I promise I'm not trying to put anyone in danger. I've spent my whole time here trying to keep people safe. This place..." he trailed off and shivered. "It's not right."

Tabitha considered his words. To them, he had been trapped in that world for a long time, but to him, it had only been a short while. Even though he knew plenty about the strange dimension, he might not have had time to learn everything. Tabitha dropped her arms.

"I believe him."

"You do?" Lisa's voice went up an octave.

"Yeah. Remember, time moves differently here. And blaming each other isn't helping us find a way out. This place messes with your head. You said yourself it's making you a little crazy. If it gets us to turn on each other, it's over."

Monica nodded. "Makes sense." She relaxed her stance and leaned on her large stick.

"She's right," Corrie agreed. "My power only works a little bit in here, and Lisa, you have no tech. We can only rely on each other."

"Wait a minute." Hannah turned in a circle. "Where's Devin?"

"I thought he..." Tabitha trailed off as she searched the forest. Lisa gripped her stick in her hand. Corrie stood with Monica, guarding her as if she were her daughter. Eric didn't move a muscle. But Devin wasn't standing with them. Then she remembered. "He walked off into the woods with me. I saw him."

"Why didn't he come back?" Panic laced Hannah's voice.

"I don't know." Tabitha called his name. Soon, everyone joined in.

Devin had seemed so scared of the voice that called his name. What if he'd followed it to his doom? Fear jumped into Tabitha's throat.

A roar deep in the forest answered them. Eric held up a hand, signaling everyone to be quiet. Tabitha tensed. When a monster didn't crash through, she relaxed a little.

"You said other people wandered off," Lisa said to Eric. "Do you think Devin did the same?" She echoed the same questions running around in Tabitha's head.

"He heard the voice like I did." Tabitha wrapped her arms around her middle. Fear crawled along her spine. "Maybe he didn't break out like I did?" The thought made her sick. "Oh, God. Did I leave him behind?"

"You can't think like that." Eric rested a hand on her shoulder. "Did you see him near you?"

"No. I was alone."

"Then you can't blame yourself."

"I know I can't." Tabitha sighed. "But I feel guilty. When

he told me about the voice, he looked scared. Terrified." She kicked at the dirt. "I hate that he might have faced that entity alone." She fell against a tree. "We need to search for him."

"But I thought we were searching for Amanda," Corrie said.

"We can't leave a man behind." Lisa brandished her stick.

"What do we do now?" Monica asked.

"There's six of us." Eric took the lead. "Three of us can hunt for Devin while the other three continue to look for Amanda. We can mark this place and meet back here."

"I think that's the best plan," Tabitha agreed.

"Wait." Corrie held out a hand, her blue eyes taking on a glassy look.

"Corrie? Are you picking up on something else?" Lisa moved closer.

Tabitha followed her oldest sister's lead and walked to Corrie.

Corrie met Tabitha's eyes. "Tristan's dad is back. He wants to talk to you."

23

Are you up for it?" Tabitha's heart jumped. Maybe Aaron had news or a way out.

Corrie nodded and closed her eyes. When she reopened them, her whole body straightened. Her gaze sharpened. "Tabitha?" Her thicker accent indicated Tristan's father had replaced Corrie.

"Mr. Johnson?" Tabitha learned not to take anything for granted in the forest, even if the answer seemed obvious.

"Yeah. Corrie and I can't hold this connection for long. I've got to tell you something."

Flutters danced in Tabitha's stomach. "What is it? Have you learned anything else?"

"Aaron went through the portal."

Tabitha stumbled back. Both excitement that he landed in the forest and fear for his safety warred inside of her. Lisa steadied her.

"When?" Lisa asked when Tabitha couldn't.

"Last night. It's been at least ten hours on our side. I don't know how long that is for you."

"I never heard the portal open." Eric pressed his lips together. "We must be farther away."

"He could be anywhere." Fear overtook every other emotion. It bubbled and twisted inside of Tabitha. "He could be dead." First, the entity snatched Devin, and now Aaron wandered around the forest alone.

"He's tougher than you think." Lisa tightened her grip. "You have to believe in him, Tabby."

"One more thing before Corrie loses me." Corrie as Mr. Johnson held up a hand. "We think someone, or something, helped Amanda along to her death. Tristan pieced parts of it together. Said he heard a strange voice luring Amanda to the water."

"What does that mean?" Monica asked.

Tabitha steadied herself as the information sank in, pushing past her fear for Aaron. She had to stay rational and clear-headed. "It means the demon killed her without the portal. Her death might have caused it."

"Now I've got a million more questions for her." Tabitha detected the hard edge in Lisa's voice.

"I have to go, but if Corrie will let me, I'll check in when I have the strength."

"Thank you," Tabitha said.

Corrie's eyes closed again. She sagged, and Eric caught her before she hit the ground. After a few minutes, her eyes fluttered open. "That takes so much out of me here." She leaned against Eric and smiled. "It's worth it, though, to keep in touch with the outside world."

"That was one of the weirdest things I've ever seen," Eric held on to Corrie.

"You mean the coolest," Monica stared at Corrie with wide eyes.

"Thank you, Corrie. I mean that," Tabitha said, love filling her heart, and her eyes welling.

Corrie took her hand. "Don't cry, silly. I'm okay."

"I know you're okay, but still." Tabitha took a breath, blinking the tears back. Everything hit her all at once—being away from home, watching Corrie's power drain her, and knowing Aaron walked in this nightmare forest searching for her. An arm curled around her waist. Lisa pulled her close.

"Tabby's right. I've never really paid attention to how much it takes out of you to channel. But now I realize."

"You guys. You're going to make me cry."

"As touching as all of this is, we need to move." Hannah stepped between them with Monica right behind her. "We can't stay in one place for too long."

"Hannah's right. We don't have the clearing to hide in anymore," Eric agreed. He looked down at Corrie. "Can you walk?"

Corrie nodded. "I'm feeling better. I think I can manage."

"We can help her," Tabitha reached for her sister.

Eric passed Corrie to her sisters and moved away.

"So, what now?" Monica asked.

"What do you mean?" Hannah brushed a fallen leaf off her shoulder.

"Corrie said someone new came through the portal. We need to find him."

"We also need to help Devin and find Amanda to get some answers," Eric said. "So, I suggest we drop down to teams of two."

Lisa raised her hand. "Okay, I call..."

The ground rumbled under their feet, cutting off her response. Everything around them shook and rattled.

"Not another one." Lisa grabbed for the nearest tree. Tabitha and Corrie stumbled along behind her until all three were wrapped around a giant tree trunk.

"Hold on!" Eric yelled as the rumbling grew louder.

Around her, Tabitha saw the rest of the party hold onto the nearest trees. A cracking and tearing sounded behind her. She turned in time to see a tree tip forward and head straight for her.

Tabitha shut her eyes and swung around her trunk. The tree swooshed by her with a cold blast of air in her face. It crashed beside her. Then the ground stopped shaking. She opened her eyes to see the large fallen tree right next to her.

Why did this place seem to focus on her? Trees fell near her, monsters came after, and the dark entity expressed so much interest. The last part scared her the most.

She glanced around at the others in the forest. Out of all of them, why her? Lisa was the oldest, the strongest. She could build anything and make it work. Corrie had the power to channel souls. She acted as a bridge between the living and the dead. Wouldn't the portal and the entity be most interested in her?

But, for some reason, everything focused on Tabitha. She dug her nails into the hard tree bark, tired of the near misses and the attention. She'd reached her wit's end with this place.

Lisa grabbed her shoulder, and Tabitha jerked. "You okay?"

"Yeah." Tabitha nodded, focusing on the present. "I think so." She checked her arms, legs, and everywhere for any scratches or scrapes. She didn't find anything. She blew out a breath as she tucked her hair behind her ears. She was tired of all the running and hiding and fighting. She didn't know how Eric had done it all this time. Then she remembered it hadn't felt like years to him. Still, she didn't think she could make it much longer. She leaned against the tree.

"Maybe we should give up."

Lisa lifted her head. "Give up?"

"We don't know what we're doing here. We don't even know what here is."

Corrie reached out a hand. "But Aaron is here. We have to find him."

"And then what? There's no way out." Everywhere she looked, she saw gray sky and dark bare trees with spindly dead limbs. Crunchy leaves littered the ground, and not one animal sound filled the quiet. "Damn it, Lisa. Why didn't you think of a way out before you jumped in?"

Lisa jammed her hands into her jacket. "I wasn't thinking. I just wanted to know how it operated." She shrugged and kicked at a leaf. "The legend behind portals is that they let things like ghosts or demons out. Or that they transport you back in time. But this one sucked things in. I wanted to know why." She peered at the treetops. "And why did Amanda work so hard warning people away?"

"Not did," Corrie said. "*Does*. She still tries to keep people away." She sighed. "We now know the answer to that question. She doesn't want people to get stuck here."

"And we're back to the original plan." Monica stuffed her hands in her pockets, a sullen expression on her face. "Does anyone have anything to eat or drink?"

Lisa pulled a bundle out of her pocket. She unwrapped it, revealing berries of different colors. "I tried one. They're safe."

Everyone plucked a couple. Tabitha tasted the sweet and juicy fruit on her tongue. It lifted her spirits, for the moment. Eric provided refilled bottles of water, handing one to each person.

"Now, who's on which team?" Lisa pulled back her shoulders, her expression serious.

"Obviously, I'm on Team Amanda." Corrie stepped to the side. "I can still try to sense her."

Eric nodded. "I'll go with Tabitha to find her husband."

"I'm not leaving my baby sister alone with you. I'm coming, too." Lisa set her jaw.

"Teams of two, remember? Go with Corrie. Get those answers," Tabitha said.

"Then that means Monica and I will look for Devin." Hannah stepped forward.

"Good. Let's go." Tabitha balled her fists and set off in a random direction.

"Wait!" Eric's voice stopped her. "We need a meeting point." He pulled one of his arrows out and stuck it into the nearest tree. "Leave something behind you to create a trail, and we'll meet back here."

"And if one of us can't make it back?" Monica asked, her voice trembling.

"I'll find you." Corrie's mouth firmed. "I can sense you, remember? Something about this place makes me more focused. I'll find you."

"Then it's settled. We meet back here." Nerves fluttered in Tabitha's stomach. She didn't like the idea of Corrie and Lisa going in a different direction without her.

"Good luck." Corrie pulled both of her sisters into a hug. "Please be careful."

"We will. Damn, I wish we'd brought our walkie-talkies." Tabitha tightened her hold.

Tabitha closed her eyes. After years of not talking, it felt good to be with her sisters again. It felt good to not fight with them. She didn't know if they'd all survive, nor if they'd all be this close when they got back to the real world, but she held on to the moment as tightly as she could.

When Lisa and Corrie let go, Tabitha pivoted. Taking a deep breath, she and Eric chose one direction while Corrie and Lisa chose another. Hannah and Monica chose a third option. They traversed a few steps when the bushes all around them rustled. Eric froze and held out a hand. Tabitha stopped. The world erupted into screams.

"Corrie! Lisa!" Tabitha ran back to the meeting place.

"Tabitha, wait!" Eric followed, staying close.

By the time they reached the clearing, nothing remained. "Maybe they got away." Tabitha walked the edge, finding no one.

Eric notched an arrow. "I don't think so."

The rustling began again. Tabitha stumbled back as a large shadow monster burst through the trees. More followed, appearing from every side. So many of them, all in one spot.

"Eric!" Tabitha whirled in time to see a monster pick him up. He disappeared into the shadowy folds.

"No!' Tabitha scrambled for a stick, wishing she held the bat from her earlier encounter with the demon. A hand clamped over her mouth, another grabbed her arm, and they yanked her back through the trees.

24

A cage. Someone had locked Aaron in a cage. When he woke up, he lay in the middle of a clearing the size of a perfect circle. Compacted dirt filled the empty space, with trees surrounding the edge. Groaning, he scrambled to his feet. He raced to the edge, determined to get away, and ran into an invisible wall. He fell, landing on his back, his head aching. With a growl, he tried again. He kicked, punched, and threw dirt at every part of the circle. Nothing passed through.

Why didn't anything make sense in this place?

He took a deep breath and paced the round area. Devin appeared through the trees. He pressed his hands against the barrier and curled his lip.

"Care to tell me what's going on?" Aaron growled.

Devin looked up, a big smile on his face. "When he comes to get you, he'll set me free." He lounged against a nearby tree. "I'll get to go home, like the others."

"The others?" Aaron pushed away from the barrier and sized up the man across from him. "All the people who came through that portal never came back, Devin. I don't know who you're talking about, but he didn't let anyone go back to the real world."

"Such lies," a deep voice hissed. The trees near Devin parted on their own. A tall dark figure stepped through, stopping at the edge of the clearing. He both looked and didn't look human with his dark hair and pale skin. Black eyes narrowed at Aaron. He curled his lip. "You're the one the woman loves so much. You disgust me."

Aaron stumbled back a couple of paces. He swallowed. Inside, he shook, but he tried not to show it.

"Who are you?"

"How do you know I'm not a figment of your imagination? Lesser things have killed the poor souls who wandered in here." The man walked the perimeter, trailing his fingers along the barrier.

Aaron took another deep breath to keep his temper and his fear in check. He wanted to take out this being, but the "how" eluded him. He tried to remember all the paranormal creatures he'd met, but none fit this one. Plus, he already spent most of his energy trying to break out of the cage.

"I don't, but you also don't look like anyone I know personally."

The stranger stopped. "But you have seen Devin before, right?"

"Weird way of putting it, but yes." A cold chill slid down his spine. "If he wanted to kill me, I'd be dead now."

The stranger chuckled. "I suppose so." He nodded to the redhead. "Devin, make sure our other guests have arrived."

"Yes, sir." Devin ran into the forest, leaving Aaron alone with the stranger.

Aaron remembered Drew's theory, a theory he kicked around, too. "You're a dark entity, aren't you?"

"Your wife called me a demon, but I suppose both fit." The stranger resumed walking the outer edge of the clearing.

"But neither, if they're real, are human. How do you look so human?"

"Practice." He stopped and spread his arms wide. "With each soul that passed through here, I learned more and more about humans. What they think, what they feel." He pinned Aaron with a glare. "What they fear." He pressed his hands to the barrier. Small waves rippled on either side, and his hands slipped through.

Aaron backed away until he hit the other side of the cage.

The entity pulled his hands back and chuckled. "You act so strong all the time, but inside, you're scared like everyone else." He sneered as he paced around the clearing. "What if I made you the same offer I made Devin? What if I give you a way to escape death?"

"What's that?" Aaron followed the entity's circle, wary.

"You don't seem surprised."

"I've seen weirder things."

The entity stopped and faced Aaron. "Alright, then. You seem like an open fellow. Have you heard of the Greene Institute?"

"I have," Aaron responded, surprised. How did a creature in another dimension know about the Greene Institute?

"I suppose you have. Your wife is one of Philip Greene's three daughters. The heirs apparent. They are the only things he cares about, especially the youngest." The entity turned and paced in the other direction.

"How do you know about it?"

"Philip Greene woke me, long before Amanda opened my portal. A long time ago, I woke from my slumber to see a weakness in the walls of my prison." He placed his long arms behind his back. "I wanted to break out, and he wanted me out. We met at that moment. I pulled as much information from him as I could until he failed to release me." He stopped and sneered again. "He did not reach his goal."

"His goal?" Aaron didn't know as much about the history of the Greene Institute as he would've liked. The general history, yes. But Philip Greene held his past close to his chest. He imagined the man kept this a secret from his daughters. But this revelation shook him. "I thought the Greene Institute didn't investigate until after the portal?"

The entity smiled, showing a row of terrifying teeth. "That was the second time, and I sensed the Greene sisters then. They don't know it, but they're my way out of this world. Especially Tabitha."

Aaron dared to move closer, his heart pounding. "I don't understand. Tabitha doesn't have the tech or the ability to bring you through."

"In due time. As soon as our guests arrive." The entity closed his eyes and drew in a deep breath. "They're almost here."

Aaron didn't like this situation. Not one bit. Sure, he enjoyed the banter, but each moment inched into creepy territory. If the entity claimed he'd use Tabitha to get to the real world, Aaron would work to find a way to stop him. He needed time to plan.

And guests? Who did he expect? The thought hit him out of nowhere and fear exploded inside of him. Tabitha. Aaron doubted the demon had invited him to a barbecue. He kicked at his invisible cage again. Nothing broke, and his foot ached.

Aaron bared his teeth and pressed his hands to the clear wall. "If you lay a hand on her or her sisters, I'll kill you."

"You're in no position to do anything. I'm what you call an entity. You have no way of killing me."

At that moment, shadow monsters thudded through the forest, Devin walking ahead of them. Each one of them carried a person. Aaron's mouth went dry. As each monster approached the cage, the barrier rippled wide enough for it to dump its load. Lisa entered first, then a man Aaron had never seen before, a couple of women, and finally, Corrie followed. When the wall solidified, Aaron kneeled next to Corrie and jostled her.

Her blue eyes fluttered open. "Aaron?"

"Corrie, where's Tabitha?" His sick feeling of dread worsened.

Corrie struggled to sit. Aaron lent her a hand. "What do you mean?" She looked around the cage. "We walked in the woods together." Her breath caught as she grabbed a handful of his shirt. "She should be here."

"Let her go!" Lisa's voice rang out.

Aaron lifted his head to see Lisa getting to her feet. She fisted her hands, her brow turned down. Aaron retreated.

Corrie turned to her sister. "It's okay. It's Aaron."

"How do we know it's Aaron?" Lisa narrowed her eyes. He'd known her long enough that she'd probably skewer him, whether he was the real one or not.

The strange man Aaron didn't know stood beside her, his feet apart. "What's going on?" He flexed his fingers. The other two women flanked him.

"I can't tell if this is my brother-in-law or not, Eric." Lisa took a step closer, her fists tightening.

"It is him." Corrie held out a hand, palm up. She closed her eyes for a moment before opening them again. "His spirit is warm and alive."

"It's me, Lisa. Although, you would know a demon, wouldn't you? Aren't you made out of the same material?" Aaron helped Corrie to her feet.

Lisa sneered. "I guess I have to take your word for it."

"Good." The one called Eric marched over to him. "If you came here thinking you could grab your wife and go home, think again. That's not how it works around here."

Aaron indicated the cage. "Clearly." He stood his ground. He didn't trust the stranger. "And you know how it works?"

"I've been here long enough to figure out how it doesn't work." Eric brushed past him. He placed his hands against the barrier and pushed.

Aaron stood back. He let him grunt and groan for a while. He crossed his arms over his chest. "Won't do you any good. I don't know what it's made out of, but it won't budge."

"Can all of you stop fighting for one second?" The young black woman glared at everyone in turn. She turned that glare on Lisa. "That's all you seem to do."

Lisa sneered before she banged a fist on her area.

Aaron took a deep breath. "Now," he turned back to Corrie. "Where's Tabitha?"

"I don't know." Her expression of worry nearly broke him. "She was with us, planning to find you."

"She disappeared during the fight." Lisa kicked at the invisible wall. She winced when her leg snapped back. "I thought the shadow monsters got her, too."

Aaron swallowed. He declined to think the worst. "Then she's still out there somewhere." After all, the entity wanted her alive. The entity! Remembering, he whirled around to find the thing watching him.

"No!" The entity appeared right in front of him, but outside of the cage, his face a mask of pure fury. "Only two of you are here. Where is the third one?"

"Oh, my God," the unknown, tawny-skinned woman with Eric gasped. "What the hell is that?"

"It's okay." Devin appeared beside him. "He wants the three sisters. He'll let the rest of us go."

"Devin?" Eric asked. "What's going on?"

Devin pressed his hands against the wall, his expression eager. "He's going to help us."

Eric shoved his way to the front. "Were you spying on us the whole time?" His jaw twitched.

The other two women moved closer to Eric, their eyes wide.

"Devin?" The older one asked. "Did you?"

"It wasn't spying." Devin's eyes were feverish. "I was keeping you safe. He was keeping you safe. All you have to do is join us."

The entity grabbed Devin's shirt and lifted him off the ground. "Thank you for all your help." He opened his mouth. In the blink of an eye, he bit Devin's flailing arm. Devin dissipated into black smoke. The entity opened his mouth wider and inhaled all of it.

"Shit!" Fear stabbed Aaron. He'd faced ghosts, both killers and harmless, but he never saw anything like that. Cold sweat trickled down the back of his neck.

The others stumbled back. The teenager covered her mouth while the other woman screamed. Eric whirled away, horror masking his features. Lisa and Corrie grabbed each other.

The sky around the entity darkened. Ominous clouds formed and thunder rolled. A crack of lightning sizzled too near to the clearing for Aaron's comfort. "It looks like one of the Greene sisters got away." He bared his teeth. "Guard our guests in the cage." And in the blink of an eye, he evaporated.

Trees whizzed by as Tabitha sailed through the air. She struggled against her captor, but the grip held tight. She estimated they covered miles in the span of seconds. Her stomach twisted and rolled, the motion almost too much for her. She shut her eyes, hoping that would help.

Then the motion stopped. It was so abrupt she thought her stomach left her body for a moment. Tabitha felt solid ground beneath her feet. Her captor removed their grip, and she wiped her mouth and whirled around. She wobbled and grabbed a nearby tree trunk for support.

"I'm sorry. Are you hurt?" a worried female voice asked.

When her head stopped swimming, Tabitha saw Amanda standing in front of her. The ghost appeared unchanged since the last time she saw her. Straight, dark hair parted in the middle and falling to her waist. A tight yellow, T-shirt and flared bell-bottom jeans. A pretty face with brown eyes and light brown skin that was solid as opposed to see-through.

"What happened?" Tabitha asked when she got her breath back. "Where are the others?"

"I couldn't save them, but I could save you." Amanda seemed to hide behind a tree. "If he's missing one, he won't kill the rest." She chewed her bottom lip and glanced around with a fearful look in her eyes.

"What are you talking about?" Tabitha's head buzzed. A headache bloomed behind her eyes.

"He wants you and your sisters. I don't know why." Amanda regarded her shoes.

Tabitha leaned forward, resting her hands on her knees. The flight through the forest took the wind out of her. She sucked in a slow breath. "So many monsters all in one place."

"His soldiers. He created them." Amanda turned. "I have to go."

"Oh, no you don't." Tabitha straightened and reached out, her hand meeting a solid arm. Much like it had the first time. But this time, she planned to hold on. "Tell me what's going on. Give me a fighting chance this time. I have a lot of questions for you."

"I can't." Amanda's voice cracked. "He'll know."

"Is 'he' the dark entity? The one I met?" Tabitha stretched her free arm high above herself. "About this tall? Dark hair, dark eyes, scary as hell?"

Amanda visibly shook as she nodded and wrapped her arms around herself. "He's so powerful. I've never come across anyone like that." Her voice rose an octave above a whisper. "He's a demon." She crossed herself.

Tabitha's heart ached for her. Amanda was already dead, and the stranger terrified her. She didn't blame her. After facing him twice, Tabitha's nerves quivered. She struggled to keep her own voice calm. "How did you meet him?"

Amanda lifted her head. "He called to me, even when I was alive. I tried not to listen, but it got harder."

Tabitha took the other woman's cold hands in her own. That touch alone reminded her that Amanda was dead, but she didn't let go. "Your death opened the portal, didn't it?"

Amanda nodded. "I didn't mean to. It just kind of happened." She started to relax her shoulders. "One moment I heard the voice. The next, I couldn't breathe. Too much water." She pulled her hands away and covered her face. "Part of me wanted it, but part of me didn't. I'm so embarrassed."

Tabitha took in the gray sky and dead trees around her. "What do you remember? About dying?"

"It's hard to explain." Amanda creased her brow. She paced away from Tabitha. "I liked the lake at night, even though most people said it gave them a weird feeling, especially my sister. Harry made me so mad that night. I don't remember what we fought about, but I had to get out. Get away."

Tabitha reached for her hand again. "What happened next?"

"I walked around the lake for a long while. And then I heard the voice."

"Did you hear it any of the other times?"

"No." Amanda shook her head. "I heard it so clearly that night. I looked down at the water and felt this urge to jump in." Her eyes took on a far-off look. "I can't swim, but before I knew it, I went under." Tears pricked the edges of her eyes. "I struggled to breathe. I fought and kicked. But everything darkened."

She faced Tabitha. "I woke up here. It must be hell because the monsters came for me. *He* came for me. He took one look at me, thanked me, and disappeared."

Something growled in the distance. Amanda tensed. "I have to go."

"I'm coming with you." Tabitha tightened her grip.

"I can't take you with me." Amanda yanked her hand away.

"Why not?"

"Because you can't go outside like I can." She sobbed. "When he grabbed the first one that came through the portal after I died and then killed her, I saw him drink her soul. That's the only way I can describe it." Horror crossed her face. "I ran through the portal and appeared at the lake. When I learned I could go back and forth, I tried to keep people away. I didn't want them to die like that."

"And when you couldn't keep them away, you created the clearing."

Amanda placed a hand on her heart. "It took so much energy, but I had to protect them. Protect you."

The growl sounded again. Amanda jumped, threatening to run again. "Please, I have to go."

"If you leave me here, he'll find me." Her words stopped Amanda's retreat. "You saved me for a reason." Tabitha touched her arm again. "Why does he want me?"

"I don't understand it, but I've heard him say you and your sisters are the key. I don't know what that means. I'm sorry." Amanda hung her head for a moment before lifting it. She held out her hand. "I can take you to the edge. We'll be safe there for a little while."

Tabitha grabbed her hand. "I'll take it."

She lost her breath as Amanda pulled her along another whirlwind trip through the forest. Amanda moved so fast that Tabitha barely had time to get her thoughts in order.

And then the movement stopped. When Amanda let go, Tabitha bent over and worked to catch her breath. Her stomach did another flip, threatening to toss up the few berries she had eaten earlier.

The current investigation topped the charts as the strangest. An aware ghost created a safe place in a world

189

controlled by a dark entity. She'd never come across anything like that in the books and websites she read, or on any investigation she had ever been a part of. How? How did Amanda defy him?

With all the research she had studied, she continued to learn new things about ghosts. Based on her experiences, Tabitha knew if a person experienced an emotion strong enough when they died, it kept their energy or soul anchored to the world of the living. The White Lady in Tristan's apartment building had a strong sense of vengeance against the men she believed were responsible for her death. A fiddle connected to Drew's family housed two ghosts, one filled with hate, and one filled with love.

But Amanda presented a whole new mystery. She drowned, but somehow, she stayed anchored to the lake. She didn't seem angry or hateful. She loved, but it didn't seem to be the reason she held on. She wanted to protect people from the portal. A portal Tabitha knew her father would love to get his hands on.

Tabitha suspected for a long time that her father didn't really care about the ghosts. Their potential captivated him. If people harnessed this kind of power after death, he wanted to know how to harness it in life.

"Are you okay?" Amanda's question broke into Tabitha's thoughts.

Tabitha straightened, her breathing back to normal. "I will be. Thank you."

"Don't thank me yet. We probably don't have much time." Amanda peered out of the trees.

Now that she had time to see her surroundings, Tabitha noticed they were in a small clearing, barely big enough for two people. Not much light came through the trees above her, the trees that were bent overhead like a roof.

"The trees hide me when I need them to." Amanda turned back to Tabitha.

"Please don't take this the wrong way, but how are you possible? How is all of this possible?" Tabitha walked the perimeter of the tiny circle.

"I don't know. I honestly don't." Amanda wiped her hands on her jeans.

Tabitha tucked her hair behind her ears and tried to gather her thoughts. "What did you feel when you died?"

"Fear. Hurt. The fight with Harry was my fault." Her hand flew to her mouth. "It was my fault. All of it. If I hadn't said anything, we'd be okay. I wouldn't have come to the lake. There'd be no portal."

"Guilt. You feel guilty." Tabitha sucked in a breath as the realization dawned on her. "And guilt usually leads to punishment." Puzzle pieces clicked into place. "The demon likes doubt, and guilt brings a lot of doubt."

But Amanda blocked her out. She started rocking back and forth. "I don't deserve to be here. I deserve much worse. All those people, dead or trapped because of me." As she spoke, the trees closed in tighter.

Tabitha touched her shoulder. "Breathe. Calm down."

"Don't you understand?" Amanda pushed her fingers back through her hair, tension on her face. "Everything is my fault!"

The whole world shook, and the ground beneath them split apart.

A manda, you have to calm down. Please." Tabitha jumped away as the ground cracked apart.

Amanda rocked on the other side, her knees drawn to her chest and her whole body shaking. "My fault. My fault."

In that moment, Tabitha thought she'd broken the ghost. What if she brought down the world with everyone trapped inside? It was yet another example of her terrible skills as an investigator. The ground rattled and rumbled. Tabitha grabbed the base of a tree, giving herself time to think.

But she didn't have time to think. Amanda rocked on the ground. Her friends, and possibly Aaron, had vanished. She hoped no one was dead. The trees around her tumbled down.

No, she refused to wimp out and hope someone rescued her. Not this time. She let go of the tree trunk and crawled on her hands and knees to the crack. She crept, balancing her way across. She glanced up, hoping nothing would fall on her. When she reached the crack, and Amanda on the other side, she gathered her strength.

"Amanda! Stop it!" she yelled.

She didn't think it would work, and it didn't. Tabitha took a breath.

"Listen! None of this is your fault. Whether that voice talked you into it, or you slipped into the water, it was an accident. You didn't plan this." Amanda stopped shaking and lifted her head. The ground stilled.

"Every couple fights. I fought with my husband before I came here. He still followed me." Tabitha crawled closer. "I've also been terrible at my job." She reached the edge and stopped. "You see, I grew up investigating the paranormal, primarily ghosts. I do that for a living now. And I've probably messed up more cases than I've solved. But you can't let the guilt eat you. The only person who will blame you in the end is yourself.

"I'll bet the lives lost in this place aren't your fault, either. No one blames you." She rested a hand on Amanda's arm. "You created the clearing, remember?"

Amanda nodded.

"It kept everyone safe for as long as they stayed there. You were protecting them."

"It still didn't help."

"It did. You can't make people stay, though. They chose to try and leave. You can't blame yourself for what happened to them. Same goes for when they came through the portal. You tried to stop them." The crack between them stitched itself together, inch by inch. Dirt, rock, and grass repaired itself. Tabitha crawled across the solid, safe ground. She breathed a sigh of relief as she sat down next to the ghost. "Did you create the monsters and the shadows and the people from our past?"

"No." Amanda shook her head as she wiped her eyes. "No, he did."

"Why?"

Amanda's brow wrinkled. "He said he needed energy to

stay alive, and his monsters and stuff helped him collect energy."

"I guess fear creates that energy, especially the fear you feel right before you die." Tabitha thought for a moment. "We need to stop him."

Amanda huddled next to her, a scared sixteen-year-old girl. "How do you stop a demon?" She crossed herself again.

"I don't know, but we need to find him, Amanda. I think he has my sisters and the others. This has to end." Tabitha pushed down the terror building inside of her. Amanda had asked the right question. How did one stop a demon? She reflected on everything she'd ever read or heard about dark entities. The religious named prayer as the answer, but religion never factored into Tabitha's life.

"He doesn't kidnap. He kills."

"Still. You said you saved me because he wants all three, my sisters and me." Tabitha let go of Amanda, her choice made. She stood and brushed off the dirt. "Then that's what he'll get."

"Don't." Amanda scrambled to her feet. "He'll kill you."

"He could, but I might have a chance if you come with me."

Amanda's eyes widened in fear. "I can't."

"You can. Remember the clearing. You can affect things in this world. You don't want to spend forever running from him, do you?"

"No. But..."

"No buts. I think we both have to do this together."

"And how do we stop him when we find him?"

Tabitha hadn't figured out that part of the plan. She didn't think she had that much time. He wanted her and her sisters for some purpose, and he refused to fail.

"I don't know, but we have to do something. My sisters,

my husband, and the rest are out there somewhere. I can't leave them alone."

Amanda hugged herself. "I know where they are." She straightened. "I'll take you to them."

Before Tabitha could thank her, Amanda was whisking her through the woods again.

AARON DROPPED TO THE GROUND, EXHAUSTED FROM TRYING TO break free. The last earthquake almost leveled several trees, and most of them were poised above the cage. Maybe the barrier would hold them if they fell, but he didn't want to take that chance. Everyone inside tried to break through the wall, but no one had any luck. Thankfully, the ground no longer shook, and silence covered the forest.

"I can't believe we can't get out of something we can't see." Lisa kicked one of the sides for good measure.

"Did you know all of this is because of you, Corrie, and Tabitha?" Aaron asked as he walked around the circle, searching for a weak spot.

"What do you mean?" Lisa's tone was sharp.

Aaron sighed and faced her. "The entity knows about the Greene Institute. Before a portal ever opened, your dad investigated the area. I don't know if he knew it or not, but he connected to the entity, and it learned a lot about him."

Color drained from Lisa's face. She widened her dark blue eyes. "Dad knew about Laureline Lake?"

"I don't know what he knew. I just know what the demon, entity, thing told me. He seems to think you three can break him out of here."

"Shit." Lisa leaned back against the barrier.

Corrie joined her and wrapped an arm around her. "The demon thinks we can free him? How?"

"It doesn't matter." Lisa lifted her head, anger in her eyes. "We're not helping him." She whirled and kicked at the invisible wall as hard as she could.

"I can't believe I'm going to die because of some crazy guy who's hunting you!" Monica's voice rose on the last word.

"Oh, it's not just you. We all are." Hannah glared at Lisa and Corrie from her spot across the cage.

"You'd think Dad would've told us about this." Corrie sank to the ground and sat cross-legged, her back to another section of the barrier.

"Dad? The man who never tells anybody anything? I'm not surprised." Lisa jumped for the roof of the cage, but her fingers brush air. She sank to the ground. "I'm sorry."

"For what?" Corrie asked.

Lisa rubbed her brow. "Before our first investigation, I found a small file on Laureline Lake."

"Yeah, the ghost and the portal. That's what we based our search on."

"No. It didn't mention the ghost or the portal. It only mentioned strange readings and a weakened spot between two trees." Lisa sighed. "The date was February 27, 1974."

Corrie narrowed her eyes. "A few days before Amanda died. You're telling me this now and not four years ago?" Aaron flinched. He'd never heard that hard tone in Corrie's voice before.

Eric abandoned his fight with the barrier and walked to Lisa. "What are you talking about?"

"I didn't think anything of the note at the time. Yeah, it was in Dad's handwriting, but he wrote a ton of notes in other files, too. He was a young investigator back then, maybe twenty years old." Lisa groaned. "I should've paid more attention."

Aaron looked from one sister to the other. "Can someone clue me in?"

Lisa lifted her head. "I bet Dad did something to that weak spot. Attracted the entity somehow."

"Wait." Corrie held up a hand. "Are you saying you think Dad created the portal?"

Lisa tapped her chin, a thoughtful expression on her face. "No. The portal didn't appear until after Amanda's death."

Aaron snapped his fingers. "That's it." All eyes turned to him. "Philip weakened it enough that somehow Amanda's death ripped it open." He pressed his lips together. "And how convenient for him to leave that information out of the current file."

Lisa punched the ground. "I didn't stumble on the Laure-line Lake portal. He practically gave it to me."

"He knew you'd be curious enough to find out how to get on the other side."

"God, I'm so stupid!"

"Hey." Eric laid a hand on Lisa's shoulder. "No, you're not." Lisa rested her hand over his and turned into his shoulder.

Aaron grunted. "I can't say I'm surprised. Philip Greene wants to know how the supernatural works, no matter the consequences. He sends people into the field without all the information they need. Of course, he'd try to open a portal to another world. It doesn't matter if it might hold a demon that could rip through our world."

Lisa laughed bitterly. "He'd want to own and control the demon. He'd want the demon's power."

"I don't think Dad could control the thing we saw," Corrie said.

"But he'd try."

"Well, whatever this entity is planning, he doesn't have all three of you. Maybe Tabitha can avoid him long enough for us to come up with a plan." Aaron's shoulder slumped. He was tired of the arguing, tired of the cage, tired of everything. He hoped Tabitha stayed safe somewhere out in the strange forest. She had avoided the entity this long. How about a little while longer? He tried to create a plan he could execute.

Unfortunately, everything he attempted hadn't work. The cage had no weak spots. It encompassed every round curve of the clearing. Everyone inside had tried everything they knew to do. Nothing worked. Hannah tried to talk to the large shadow monsters guarding the cage, but they didn't seem to hear her.

Aaron had to admit that he'd never faced a creature like this before. Give him a regular ghost in a haunted house, and he could figure out what to do. But a dark entity that created a whole world and sucked him inside of it? He found it hard to process something this far out of normal.

He shouldn't have jumped into the portal. He should've stayed on the other side, finding clues to pass along to Tabitha through Matthew and Corrie. But he couldn't stand it. The idea of Tabitha stuck here, fighting off who knew what, terrified him. They had faced some frightening and threatening ghosts together. No wonder she wanted to leave ghost hunting far behind her.

"Hey!" Aaron's head shot up when he heard the whisper behind him. "Aaron!" He whirled around. A cluster of brush swished right behind him. Now the bushes spoke to him? Right when he thought he lost his mind, two of the bushes parted to reveal Tabitha.

He pressed his palms against the cold invisible wall. "What are you doing here?" He struggled to keep his voice to a whisper. "Hide. Before he finds you."

Another face appeared next to Tabitha. He recognized Amanda immediately. "That's what I told her."

Tabitha nodded to the two guards. "I'm going to distract them while Amanda tries to get you out of there."

"No." He pushed all his weight against the barrier, fear spiking.

"Yes."

"Who are you talking to?" Lisa walked up next to him. She sucked in a breath. "Tabitha!" Her voice echoed.

Tabitha shushed her, but not quick enough. Everyone in the cage crowded around Aaron. He rolled his eyes. So much for the element of surprise. He glanced behind him. The shadow monsters hadn't moved from their tree trunks. He nodded to Tabitha. "I don't like the idea of you getting too close to those things."

Tabitha arched a brow. "Do you want to get out of there or not?"

"Be careful," Corrie chimed in.

Aaron tried to swallow down his fear as he watched his wife tip toe out of the brush and around the cage. He hated this idea with every fiber of his being.

Tabitha rested a hand on her stomach, hoping to calm the nerves fluttering inside. Maybe Amanda should've been the distraction. No, she had a feeling the monsters might react more to her. As she came around the curve of the clearing, she remained in the cover of the trees. When she reached the place where the monsters stood guard, she walked out into the open. She took a deep breath. Plastering on a smile, she sauntered to the nearest guard.

"Excuse me, can you help me find my way back to the portal? I think I'm lost." She ran a hand through her hair and cocked her head to the side for good measure.

Red eyes narrowed down at her. The thing roared and swung out with a big, meaty hand. Tabitha ducked out of the way. She stumbled backward into the forest. Her back smacked into a large tree trunk. She yelped, her upper back aching. By that time, the other guard saw her. When she noticed Amanda make it around the clearing, trying to find an opening, she ran.

Her back still smarted, but she ignored the pain. She bit

her bottom lip to distract herself. Lumbering heavy steps followed her, and she knew she had the guard's attention. She dodged past several trees, zig-zagging along the way. Then she turned right. As she made a wide circle, she watched Amanda push and knock against the barrier. She had found no way into that strange cage. The monsters' footsteps thundered closer. Tabitha picked up the pace, making another right. Her breath labored, and her legs joined her back in aching.

She glanced at the clearing again. Amanda pressed her hands against a section of the invisible wall. It rippled under her touch, and Aaron stuck his foot through. Relief gave Tabitha a burst of energy.

Tabitha angled back toward the clearing. But she lost track of the monsters. One grabbed her from behind and lifted her off her feet. His hold crushed her arms to her sides. She cried out in pain.

"No!" she wheezed. Her heart pounded in her ears, her muscles hurt, and the arms holding her continued to crush her.

"Let her go," a smooth, deep voice said.

The arms opened. Tabitha fell, landing hard. She lay there, every part of her hurting. The pain rose and dipped in waves. She closed her eyes for a moment, waiting for the end to come.

"Put her with the others."

"I don't think so." Tabitha's eyes opened at the sound of Aaron's voice. She rolled over in time to see Aaron leap onto the demon's back. He wrapped his arms around the entity's neck. The strange man turned into dark smoke, slipping out of Aaron's grasp. Aaron dropped to the ground with a thud.

The demon became solid again. He grabbed Aaron's shirt, hauling him off the ground. Opening his mouth, his sharp teeth gleamed.

"No!" Lisa yelled.

Pushing through the pain, Tabitha scrambled to the demon and kicked the back of one of his legs. Surprised, he dropped Aaron. A monster scooped Aaron up as if he were a feather and put him back in the clearing.

The edges of Tabitha's vision darkened as she lay her head on the ground. She breathed in the earthy scent of dirt and bark. A monster plucked her from her spot and shoved her into the clearing.

She collapsed on the floor, groaning and coughing. She vaguely heard other people joining her. Warm arms wrapped around her. Arms she knew would never hurt her.

It took all of her effort to look up. "Aaron?"

"It's me. It's really me." He pulled her into a soft hug.

As wonderful as it felt, a part of her realized they had to get out of that clearing. They had been so close. Tabitha pulled away and let Aaron help her to her feet. She sagged a little, leaning against him, but she remained upright.

The demon stood outside of the cage. Amanda stayed out of sight.

"Lisa, Corrie, and Tabitha Greene. I've watched you and waited for this moment." He paced back and forth, his hands behind his back. "I almost had you five years ago. You would've given me a chance to step into your world, but you," he pointed to Tabitha. "You somehow broke away from the portal, taking your sisters with you." He leered at her. "And you're the one I need the most."

"Who are you?" Lisa positioned herself in front of Tabitha.

"Your sister calls me a demon. Your brother-in-law calls me a dark entity. I'm all of those things." He stopped pacing and did an exaggerated bow. "My brothers, sisters, and I longed to be a part of your world for centuries. Millennia.

Some of them broke through, taking energy, creating chaos, but I have yet to succeed."

As she regained her strength, Tabitha nudged Lisa out of the way so she could face the demon. "How do you plan to succeed?"

The demon flashed them a brilliant smile full of razor-sharp teeth. "Your father started it that long ago night. He found a way to weaken the wall between my world and yours." He paced around the circle, his moves slow and deliberate.

Tabitha exchanged a look with her sisters. "He did?"

"He did." The demon stopped and cocked his head to side. "You know, it's hard to talk to you with this between us." He waved at the invisible barrier. His eyes lit with an idea as he turned to his monsters. "Bring the three blondes."

Before Tabitha could move, Lisa and Corrie flanked her sides. Aaron, Eric, Monica, and Hannah stood in front of them.

"You'll have to go through us." Aaron gritted his teeth.

"How touching." The demon waved a hand. "Kill them."

"No!" Fear shot through Tabitha's heart. She refused to watch other people die because of her, especially Aaron. If the demon wanted her, then he'd get her. She tried to push Aaron out of the way, but he became an immovable force. Lisa and Corrie joined in until they were able to move everyone. "Open the barrier. We'll come."

Aaron caught Tabitha's shirtsleeve. "This is a bad idea."

She yanked her shirt from his grasp. "I won't let him hurt you."

A wave rippled across a section of the invisible wall. Taking a deep breath, Tabitha walked out with Lisa and Corrie each holding one of her hands. The barrier solidified as soon as they were clear.

Whatever they faced next, Tabitha embraced the strength and support her sisters brought.

"Here we are," Corrie pulled her shoulders back.

"You going to make your move or are you going to bore us to death?" Lisa challenged, her brows drawn down.

The demon trailed a finger down the side of Lisa's cheek. She jerked away. "You're so tough yet so afraid of something happening to your sisters. Too bad you're not the one I need. Just the bonus."

Tabitha pulled away from her sisters, fighting to stand on her own. "You didn't answer my question. What did my father do?"

The demon's features filled with delight. "He had the most amazing machine. I don't know what it did, but it allowed me to come nearer, to talk to him. And then, he cut himself, and his blood helped weaken the barrier even more." The demon walked a circle around them.

"But you needed more," Corrie said.

"Yes. I tried numerous ways to finish the job, to push through. No luck, until a distraught teenaged girl offered me a chance. I convinced her to sacrifice herself, to slip under the water."

Dread filled Tabitha's stomach. "Her death opened the portal."

The demon stopped in front of them. "It did!"

"But you couldn't get out," Lisa watched him with wary eyes. "Why?"

"I don't know. The portal was supposed to be a way out, but it kept everything in. No matter. I lured people in." His eyes flashed to the group in the clearing. "And they sustained me." He licked his lips.

Tabitha swallowed. She wanted his attention away from the people in the barrier. "Why do you need me?"

He placed a finger under her chin and lifted it. "You have

a darkness in you. Something your sisters don't have. The same darkness your father had."

She trembled. "I'm nothing like my father."

"You're everything like him. You keep it locked away. I see the impatience, the curiosity, and the doubt. It's all there." He let go of her chin. "You're also the one he didn't want."

"That's not true," Corrie snapped out, moving closer to Tabitha.

Tabitha sneered. "How does that help you?"

"Your blood will give me a way out. Your sisters' blood will help sustain me in your world. A world filled with so much energy, so much pain. It's like a dream."

"And why can't you walk through your portal without me?"

"Because he can't." Amanda stood in the trees, keeping a safe distance between herself and the monsters.

"What?" Lisa asked.

"He can't. He's tried with the other people who came here. Their blood didn't affect the portal." Amanda stepped out of the shadows. Her hands shook, but she stood her ground.

"Well, that's a fun tidbit," Lisa commented.

The portal, the dimension, the demon. None of it made sense. But maybe it did. Ghosts were pure energy left behind. Psychics influenced energy to see and feel things. Why couldn't there be a malevolent form somewhere outside of the spectrum? Something dark that her father found and tried to free. How did you stop dark energy? No easy answer came to Tabitha. Unlike a ghost, with business to finish, he needed something else. And he wanted her to break all the way through because she carried her father's darkness and blood.

She felt it churning inside of her, her impatience and curiosity, her demand for answers without a thought for others. And the doubt filled her to the brim—she was never good enough. Was this the reason her father kept her around? To help open a portal and let a demon out into the world?

Tabitha glanced at Amanda: a heartbroken sixteen-year-old girl who might have lived if the demon hadn't taken advantage of her. But she, like Tabitha, showed more strength than she thought she had. The girl figured out how to affect things in this world and to spoil the demon's plans.

The inklings of a plan formed in her mind. A longshot, but one she had to take.

Tabitha stepped forward. "What if I make you a deal?"

"Tabitha?" Corrie's voice trembled.

"What are you doing?" Lisa's voice held steady with a warning.

"I'm saving your life." She faced the demon. "You say you need me most of all. If that's true, then I should be enough. Let everyone else go. I'll stay."

"The hell you will!" Tabitha heard a *thunk* behind her. She turned to see Aaron pound his fists against the barrier.

"Intriguing." The demon studied all three sisters. "You are the one I'm most interested in." He tapped his chin as he considered. "Done." He turned to his monsters. "They're free to spend the rest of their lives in my forest. No more hunting."

Tabitha's head snapped up. Confusion pushed through. "Wait. We made a deal."

"Yes, we did. You asked me to let them go, and that's what I'm doing." He waved his hand. The invisible walls rippled.

Aaron put out an arm, and it passed through. The group streamed out but didn't scatter. Instead, they surrounded the demon and Tabitha. Aaron laced his fingers through hers.

"You take her. You take me."

The demon curled a hand around Aaron's throat and lifted him off the ground. The force broke Aaron's connection to Tabitha. "I can't kill you, but I can hurt you a great deal."

"Let him go!" Tabitha yelled. Pieces of her plan fell apart. Aaron wasn't supposed to try and save her. He was supposed to go, taking everyone else with him. She needed Aaron to be safe. To be free.

She tried to think, to figure out how to save this idea.

"He's not worth anything to you." Tabitha grabbed the demon's arm. His icy skin froze her fingers, but she held on. "Your deal is with me and hurting him is not part of the deal. If you hurt him, you get nothing."

The demon growled, his fingers squeezing Aaron's neck. Aaron kicked and struggled. His eyes rolled back into his head. Tabitha's stomach twisted.

"Enough!" Amanda's voice echoed throughout the space. She stamped her foot, and the ground shook.

Tabitha released the demon. She moved to her hands and knees as trees crashed around them. The demon released his hold on Aaron, who landed with a groan. Tabitha scurried to him. He wrapped his arms around her, and they huddled together. She buried her face into his shoulder, wondering if she'd reached the end. She'd rather be with Aaron than anywhere else.

"I'm sorry." Aaron pitched his voice above the rumbling.

"For what?" Tabitha yelled back.

"For everything. For not listening to you. For arguing." He pulled her tighter. "If we make it through this, I'm never letting you go."

"Good. Because I'm not letting you go, either."

As quick as it started, the shaking stopped. Tabitha lifted her head. The trees around them were on the ground. The monsters were gone, leaving no trace. The rest of the group lay on the ground but seemed untouched. In the center, Amanda and the demon faced off.

"You're getting better at controlling these tantrums." The demon advanced. "But you won't trouble me any longer." He grabbed Amanda's arm and opened his mouth. He bit her. Nothing happened. He bit again. Still nothing.

"What's going on?" Tabitha asked.

"I think he's trying to kill her like he did Devin, but it's not working." Aaron stood. He offered his hand and helped Tabitha to her feet.

"I'm already dead." Amanda yanked her arm out of his grasp.

Tabitha crossed to them. "Amanda?"

"You were right. I can affect things here." She kept her gaze on the demon. He hissed and backed away. "Which means no one else has to die."

A bright, warm glow appeared around Amanda. As she placed her hand in Tabitha's, warmth spread through Tabitha's arm and traveled throughout her whole body. "You told me none of this is my fault. None of it is your fault, either. You're stronger than you think, Tabitha. Remember, he needs you."

Tabitha blinked and shielded her eyes against the bright light. "What are you saying?"

"I'm ready to go. I'm not afraid anymore, and I think the portal will go with me."

"But what about us?"

"You can send everyone home before I leave."

"What? But I'm not special. I'm sure Lisa or Corrie..."

Amanda shook her head. "No, you. I understand now. Your father started this. You can end it."

"But I don't even know what he did." Tabitha pressed a hand to her stomach. Confused, Tabitha clutched Amanda's hand. She planned to sacrifice herself and save everyone else but not let the demon out to play.

Amanda straightened, her shoulders back. She held her head high and squeezed Tabitha's hand. "Your blood may be enough to open the portal the other way." Amanda plucked a stick from the ground, one with a sharp end. She offered it to Tabitha.

"But what about the demon?"

The demon cowered away from the light, hissing and baring his teeth.

"I'll take care of him." She placed the stick in Tabitha's free hand. "Save yourself."

When Amanda let go, she took the warmth with her.

"Why didn't my blood open the portal when the monster scratched me?" Tabitha asked Amanda. Amanda didn't answer, but Tabitha thought she understood. "Intention. It's not just the blood. I have to choose to offer my blood. It's my choice."

Tabitha met Aaron's eyes. Before he moved, she pricked her finger. She gasped at the sharp pain. She let a drop hit the ground. The air around them shifted. Tabitha waited. It took a moment or two, but the lights danced in front of her. They circled and circled until the portal appeared out of nowhere. She dropped the stick and stood back.

"Now what?" Monica stared at the portal.

"Go through," Tabitha said.

Monica squared her shoulders and jumped. Hannah followed her.

Tabitha hung onto Aaron and looked around at Eric and her sisters. She then glanced at Amanda. The determined ghost advanced on the demon.

"Well, it looks like someone is a little more confident," Tabitha smiled.

Eric and Lisa held hands as they leaped through. Then Corrie went, leaving Tabitha and Aaron.

"Do you think we should do something?" Aaron asked.

"I think she's got it." Clutching his hand, Tabitha and Aaron hopped into the portal.

This time it didn't pull her through. Instead, she floated,

riding each swirl. She tumbled out of the whirling colors and into the dark, moon-filled night. When she hit the ground, it knocked the breath out of her. The portal snapped shut behind her.

Pushing herself upright, she noticed she still held Aaron's hand. He rolled over, cupped her face with his free hand, and kissed her. All the pain and the worry melted away. She pulled him closer, deepening the kiss.

"Please get a room," Lisa said.

With a laugh, Tabitha came up for air. "You'll have to deal with it."

A blue glow a couple of feet away caught her attention. Amanda appeared, a smile on her face.

"Amanda?" Tabitha stumbled toward her.

Amanda flicked her eyes to Corrie as she approached them.

"I think she wants to say goodbye." Corrie nodded to the ghost. With a smile, the blue glow merged with her. Corrie closed her eyes for a moment. When she opened them, they were filled with hope. She clutched Tabitha's hands.

"Thank you. I hoped I could say goodbye."

"The demon?" She glanced behind her, terrified she might have brought him through.

"Licking his wounds."

"Really?"

Corrie nodded. "Yeah. And I think when I leave, the portal will go with me."

"I hope so."

Corrie smiled as she closed her eyes. Amanda's blue form appeared beside her. Corrie opened her eyes and leaned against her sister for support.

"Ready?" Tabitha directed her question to Amanda.

Amanda lifted one side of her mouth in a half-smile and nodded. A light glow surrounded her body. It grew brighter and brighter until it engulfed her. When she beamed with nothing but light, she burst into a million tiny stars.

Tabitha lowered her hand, letting her eyes adjust to the darkness again.

"Tabby?" Aaron wrapped his arms around her middle. "Are you okay?"

"Yeah." Tabitha nodded. "I think so. How's everyone else?"

"We're here!" Lisa's voice rang out.

Tabitha turned. She saw everyone else coming to join them. "Well, this looks like Laureline Lake." She tucked a strand of hair behind her ear. As she did so, she noticed her finger no longer bled. In fact, the skin appeared unbroken. "What year is it?" She dug in her pockets and pulled out her cell phone. A phone that had been useless for a long time.

The display popped on showing that a week and three days had passed. She had been in the portal for a week and a half. It only felt like a few days to her. She pulled up McKenna's number and dialed.

McKenna picked up on the first ring. "Tabitha?"

"We're home. Can you come get us?"

"Stay there. We're on our way."

As Tabitha and Aaron waited for their team to arrive, everyone pulled out their own cell phones and checked to see if they still worked. Hannah cried as the call went through and she spoke to her family. Monica bounced up and down, recounting the whole adventure on hers. Eric huddled with Lisa off to the side, his phone to his ear. An unspoken connection passed between the two of them. Corrie sobbed as she talked to her daughter.

Aaron told Tabitha what happened to Devin. Her heart broke at the thought of losing one of them. The demon had taken him in, much like he tried to do with Tabitha. Devin believed him. It cost him his life. No matter what Devin had done, he didn't deserve to die that way.

"I think we should put together a memorial for him and all the others who died in that portal." Tabitha squeezed Aaron's hand. "Somebody has to remember them."

"I agree." He lifted her hand and brushed his lips across the back of it. "What I said inside the portal, I meant it."

Tabitha met his eyes. "What are you talking about?"

"I'm sorry."

"Oh." Tabitha chuckled. "Our fight. It's not important."

"It is. Tabby, this isn't a one-way marriage. I don't want my dreams to shove yours aside. If you want that job with *Western NC*, I support you, one hundred percent." He tucked a loose strand of hair behind her ear. "Your photos are amazing. The ones of the mountains in our backyard are my favorites."

Tabitha blinked. "They are?" She knew Aaron had seen her photographs, but she didn't realize he had paid attention. Her cheeks warmed at the thought.

"Well, yeah. I've got every picture you've ever taken saved on a flash drive in my desk. They calm me down when I'm upset." He grinned, his whole face brightening. The moon gave off enough light to see him. "You know, we can frame the orb pictures you take during investigations."

Tabitha laughed. "You know those are pictures of dust, right?"

"But artfully framed dust." Aaron wiggled his dark eyebrows.

Tabitha sighed. "I stared down a demon, Aaron. Something few people have ever done. It scared me to death."

"I know." Aaron pulled Tabitha closer as he rested his chin on her head. "I can't believe you tried to make a deal with him."

"I would do anything to save you."

"Yeah, well, don't do it again."

Headlights swung across the trees as a car parked as close to the lake as possible. The driver's side door popped open, and McKenna tumbled out, flashlight bobbing in her hand. "Tabitha!" She raced to the edge of the lake, bypassing everyone else and embraced her best friend.

Tabitha hugged her back, grateful. "Thank you for taking care of Aaron."

McKenna let go. "How did you know?"

"I know you."

McKenna wrinkled her nose. "True."

After everyone else received hugs and fist bumps and other people arrived to reunite with their loved ones, Tabitha and Aaron headed home to be alone.

A fter a good night's rest, Tabitha opened her eyes to sunlight streaming in through her bedroom window. For a moment, she worried she was still in the demon's twisted fantasy. She sat upright and ran a hand through her hair. She waited a beat to see if the demon as Aaron would walk through the door. No one entered.

She climbed out of bed and walked into the small living room and kitchen at the front of the house. Aaron sat at the tiny kitchen table in nothing but his pajama pants, coffee in one hand and his phone in the other.

"Good morning."

He lifted his head at the sound of her voice. A smile brightened his angular features. He set the coffee mug on the table. "Did I wake you?"

"No." Tabitha shook her head. She took a cautious step forward. "You're not planning to give up ghost hunting and go fishing, are you?"

Aaron wrinkled his nose. "Why would I do that?"

Tabitha relaxed. The house and Aaron were real. She had made it out of the portal and back home. The night before hadn't been a dream. She crossed to the table and hugged Aaron from behind.

"I love you."

"I love you more."

Feeling more like herself, Tabitha poured a cup of coffee and joined Aaron at the table. She cleared her throat, knowing the conversation she wanted to have wasn't going to be an easy one.

"We need to talk about my hours at Restless Spirits."

Aaron set his phone down. "I thought you wanted to quit."

"Well." Tabitha rested her chin in her hand. "After going through the portal, I don't think I can walk away completely."

"What do you mean?" Aaron sipped his coffee.

"I want to cut back on my hours and go for the *Western NC* job." She straightened. "I like helping ghosts find a way to let go. I liked helping the other people lost in the portal." She drank some of her coffee, sorting the words out in her mind. "Those have always been the parts about investigating I liked." She met his eyes. "The parts you brought to my life."

Aaron reached across the table and held her hand. "Are you sure? Before, you said you wanted a change. Like I said last night, I'll support whatever change you want, as long as you're still with me."

Tabitha widened her eyes. "I'll always be with you. That's not going to change, ever. But I learned you need me to get out of tight spots." A corner of her mouth curved up.

Aaron chuckled. "I guess I do. Who else is going to keep me calm?"

"We do have an empath on staff."

"You know what I mean." Aaron gave her a condescending look.

"I do." Tabitha pulled her hand away, leaned back in her chair, and enjoyed more of the rich, slightly cooled coffee.

"I'm going to leave the researching and the post-investigation work to McKenna, Tristan, and Drew. But if you need my help during an actual investigation, I'm there."

"I wouldn't have it any other way."

A week later, Tabitha settled on the couch in her living room with Lisa, Corrie, Aaron, and the rest of the Restless Spirits team. Her team, her family, and her friends. At one time, she questioned whether she wanted to continue to investigate ghosts. After the talk with Aaron, she realized she liked helping them move on. She ignored the demon's words. She accepted her dark nature, but she didn't let it consume her. If helping ghosts and saving people were the way to balance it out, then she'd do it.

But she also applied for the photography job. After talking to the magazine, she learned about the flexible hours, which were enough to let her work with Restless Spirits and do what she loved.

Studying the group of people surrounding her, Tabitha knew it was the right time to tell them.

She smiled. "I got the job."

"You did?" McKenna jumped off the other end of the couch and bounced up and down. Corrie and Lisa pulled Tabitha into a group hug.

"You're going to do so well at this," Lisa said.

"Thank you."

Tristan and Drew whooped and hollered while Aaron smiled from his chair, his pride filling the room.

"I knew you could do it," Corrie said.

Tabitha basked in the love surrounding her, but she knew she had other business to discuss with her sisters.

"How much did you tell Dad?" she asked once everyone calmed down.

"Only the bits about Amanda. He doesn't know about

Eric, Hannah, or Monica." Lisa exchanged a glance with Corrie. "They've been through enough."

"He also doesn't need to know about the entity. Although, he hasn't asked." Corrie sipped a glass of sweet tea.

"He did punch a hole in his wall when we told him the portal closed for good, though." Lisa chuckled.

Tabitha widened her eyes. "How do you know?"

"Eric and I took some equipment to the lake two nights ago. The readings came back different. The numbers were lower, so I think that's a good sign." Lisa picked up her mug of hot chocolate. "We're going to check again next March."

"Can I join you? Maybe we can build something to make sure it's closed." Drew scooted to the edge of the couch.

"I'll call you and see what we can collaborate on." Lisa clinked her mug with Drew's.

"How are the others doing?" McKenna leaned forward.

"Adjusting," Corrie answered. As Tabitha understood it, Corrie and Noah were the last to stay at the lake that night and to make sure everyone had a ride home. She said she dodged the explanation of why Hannah and Eric hadn't aged to their families. She didn't think they cared as long as they were home. "Monica's doing the best. Hannah's sister is working with her." She grinned and nudged Lisa. "Lisa offered to help Eric adjust to society again."

"Did you?" Tabitha pushed Lisa's leg with her foot. "You didn't tell me." She suspected something happened between them, but they both kept it private.

Lisa waved it away. "It's not important."

"Sure, it isn't." Tabitha sung.

Lisa rolled her eyes. "Can we talk about something else?"

Aaron tapped Tabitha on the shoulder. "Can I talk to you a second?"

"Sure."

Tabitha excused them and followed Aaron into their

bedroom. As soon as the door closed, she didn't have time to catch her breath. He swept her into a bone-deep kiss that she felt all the way to her toes. Chills broke out all over her body.

When they came up for air, Tabitha arched a brow. "What did you kiss me for?"

"Just because." Aaron grinned. "I didn't do that enough, and when I lost you, I thought I'd never do it again."

"Aaron."

"Whatever you choose to do, I support you. You're stuck with me, baby."

Tabitha drew him back down into another kiss. Her heart swelled. "I choose you, I choose the ghosts, and I choose the magazine. We're in this together." She poked his chest. "After all, you need me."

"You better believe it."

She nibbled his chin, the stubble scratchy against her lips. "I'll make you a deal."

"Yes?" He lifted her off the ground.

"If you get everybody out of this house, you'll get to see me naked."

Aaron set her feet on the ground. "I'm on it."

"Excellent."

Tabitha wanted nothing more than to spend the rest of the day with only Aaron. She'd proved her worth to him. And she'd proved her worth to her team. And she vowed not to make any more deals.

AUTHOR'S NOTE AND ACKNOWLEDGMENTS

My third book. Who knew this would happen? Thank you to everyone who bought, read, and reviewed the first two. I really appreciate it.

John Hartness and Melissa Gilbert, thank you for continuing to believe in this series and making me feel welcomed at Falstaff. If it weren't for you, I'd be telling myself these stories.

Thank you to my friends: Rachel, Susan, Tally, and Bill. You inspired the series, and it keeps growing. Rachel was the one who named Tabitha, and I've grown to love that name.

To everyone from LiveJournal: you got to read my ramblings about the first book and the world. I wouldn't have kept going if you hadn't made me icons and fanart and cheered me on. Some days, I miss that community.

Thank you to my family, who nurtured the writing from the beginning. And to all my nieces and nephews! I can't wait to see what you do in life.

Laureline Lake and its portal do not exist. That's probably a good thing, so don't go traipsing around the woods searching for it. In fact, it's probably best to stay out of the woods altogether.

This book was a hard one to write, but I think I'm most proud of it. It's my most personal to date, and it was the book I needed to write. We've been through a lot this past year, and we continue to deal with our ongoing struggles. Even when things look the darkest, there's always hope.

I hope you enjoy this latest Restless Spirits adventure.

ABOUT THE AUTHOR

Amy Ravenel has done a bit of everything – waitressing, customer service, teaching, librarianship. But writing has been the only thing she's ever wanted to do. She has a deep love for bookstores, the mountains, and all sorts of geeky things. A native North Carolinian, she grew up in the foothills near the inspiration for Mayberry. Today, she lives with her epically-bearded husband and her epically-furry cats.

You can subscribe to her newsletter at amyravenel.com or join her Facebook Group, AMY RAVENEL'S LIBRARY.

ALSO BY AMY RAVENEL

Restless Spirits Series

White Spirit
Cursed Spirit

FRIENDS OF FALSTAFF

Thank You to All our Falstaff Books Patrons, who get extra digital content each month! To be featured here and see what other great rewards we offer, go to www. patreon.com/falstaffbooks.

PATRONS

Dino Hicks
John Hooks
John Kilgallon
Larissa Lichty
Travis & Casey Schilling
Staci-Leigh Santore
Sheryl R. Hayes
Scott Norris
Samuel Montgomery-Blinn
Junkle

www.ingramcontent.com/pod-product-compliance
Lightning Source LLC
Chambersburg PA
CBHW050314110726
47899CB00007B/2231